VICTOR
IN THE
JUNGLE

For Bode —
I wish you many
great adventures!

Best,
Alex Finley

VICTOR

IN THE

JUNGLE

A SATIRE BY
ALEX FINLEY

Smiling Hippo Press

For information about this title or to order other books and/or electronic media, contact the publisher:
Smiling Hippo Press
SmilingHippoPress.com

ISBNs:
softcover: 978-0-9972510-2-9
eBook: 978-0-9972510-3-6

Printed in the United States of America
Cover and Interior design: 1106 Design

For my husband and son,
The best people to have adventures with.
Ready for the next one?
¡Vámonos!

Also by Alex Finley

Victor in the Rubble

Adult: Do you want to go for a walk?
Child: No.
Adult: Do you want to go for an adventure?
Child: Yes!

CHAPTER ONE

"It's not technically breaking the law, so don't look so worried." Victor took a big gulp of his coffee while looking Mike straight in the eye. Mike seemed to shrink in his seat. "Think of it as just another meeting. One man meeting another man to talk. Forget about the drugs and the terrorists. It's a friendly chat. A chat with a man who could incriminate a lot of people, but still, just a chat. That's all."

The bar area was empty except for the two of them and a tired-looking bartender whose shoes squeaked when he walked. The long wooden bar was scratched and splintered. Every few feet it was painted with images of palm trees, people in canoes, and the nearby volcano, Paxico, with clouds of ash spewing from its crater. The colors had probably once been bright, but now the paint was faded and chipped in places. Similar paintings lined the wall behind the bar and dirty dishes and glasses piled up on the counter below them. Victor saw a tarantula perched high up in a corner, its hairy legs and body as still as the people in the dulled paintings. A small black-and-white television, its antenna bent, burbled static quietly at the end of the bar.

CYA case officer Victor Caro and his colleague Mike Quinn sat nursing fresh watermelon juice and coffee at the bar. The bar area opened onto the lobby, which also had once been painted with luminescent greens and yellows. It was now worn down and tired from the jungle's oppressive heat, a hot misty cloud that wrapped itself around the town and never let go. Four women sat on two couches near the check-in desk. The skin of their bare legs melted and spread across the faux leather cushions, sticking and sweating, pools of perspiration collecting under their knees. Their camisoles clung to their wet skin. They didn't move, except to fan their wet, tired faces. A bright red bird darted through the lobby, landing on a curtain rod with a chirp.

"Explain it to me again," Mike said. He wiped his palms on his cargo pants, leaving a small streak.

"You've got the Revolutionary Armed Forces for the Liberation of the Formerly Free Peoples of Tamindo," Victor said.

"That's a big name," said Mike.

"The more violent they became, the more lefty words they added. We shortened it to the FRPT."

"Shouldn't it be the RAFLFFPT?" Mike asked. He pronounced it *raffle-fuh-fipt*.

"FRPT, for the group's name in Spanish."

"Firpt," said Mike.

"The FRPT," Victor said each letter separately, "has been working out of Tamindo, just north of here, for forty years. They started as your typical leftist, Marxist ideological group. *Revolución*, *la lucha*, Che and motorcycles. Until about fifteen years ago, when they realized there's not much money in ideology. But drugs . . ."

Mike nodded. "A lot of money in drugs."

"Pulu, the president of Tamindo, is actually an upstanding guy, especially since we give him lots of money to be *our* upstanding guy. But he's been a little too upstanding. He did too good a job. The FRPT realized Tamindo is kind of a hard place to work now."

"You think they're coming over to this side of the border? To Guayandes?"

"Exactly. I think the group wants to make Guayandes their new home base. That's why I'm meeting with VZSPARKLEPONY tonight."

"Your source is called VZSPARKLEPONY?"

Victor nodded.

"I've seen BTSTARSHIP and MQMERMAID. Those were cool," Mike said.

"A computer picks the name. Can we move on?"

"But VZSPARKLEPONY? That's pretty lame."

"Bottom line is, *VZSPARKLEPONY*," Victor emphasized the name, "should be able to shed some light on exactly what the FRPT's plans are here in Guayandes."

"President Evorez can't handle the border himself?" Mike swished his watermelon juice in its glass.

"Rafa Evorez." Victor almost spit out the name of the president of Guayandes. The portly leader had come to power fifteen years earlier in a coup and quickly cemented his position by rallying the country's poorest into believing he would be their savior. This required two things: developing a cult of personality around himself and creating an external enemy who posed—at least according to Evorez—an existential threat to Guayandes and her people.

He had succeeded in the first by nicknaming himself El Toro, cultivating an image of himself as a strong, virile bull. The Guayandan press was not allowed to report on any of his short-comings, because he didn't have any. When a newspaper editor once wrote a column that called El Toro a dictator, Evorez had him thrown in jail for three years, seemingly unaware he was proving the editor's point. He also was fond of repeating his poll numbers to anyone who would listen, which was everyone because El Toro's bodyguards wouldn't let anyone leave the room when he was talking. His approval rating always hovered above 80 percent, according to Guayandes' top—and only—polling firm, which was run, conveniently, by El Toro's brother.

As for the second, Evorez had managed to paint for the Guayandan people a picture of an enemy so fierce, so frightening, that the people had no choice but to place their faith and their future in his trustworthy hands. This giant menace, this *Diablo*, that threatened the very existence of Guayandes and which was behind all—yes, *all!*—of her ills had a name: the United States of America.

"Rafa Evorez doesn't *want* to handle the border," Victor said to Mike. "It's in our interest not to allow any more instability to what is already an unstable country. That's why we're here."

"Here" was Kiltoa, a remote Guayandan town buried in the never-ending green of the Amazon jungle. Kiltoa was always wet, and everything in Kiltoa was always wet. Victor knew when he went to Kiltoa that his clothes would stay humid the entire time.

He had even given in and bought a bunch of quick-dry shirts, which he had eschewed after his trips to Rubblestan and other war zones, where they seemed to be the uniform of every CYA officer. But even those never dried here, so Victor resigned himself with each trip to Kiltoa to be sticky and dirty for days. He was finding that he quite liked it.

"*Hola*, Maria."

Victor and Mike turned toward the voice in the lobby. A tall man with white hair, naked except for a tattered white bathrobe and brown flip-flops, was greeting each of the women who were stuck to the couches. "Maria," he said, kissing one on the cheek. "Maria." He kissed another. They were all named Maria.

"That's Frank Trill. He's one of our contractors," Victor said to Mike.

"I take it this isn't his first time in Kiltoa," Mike said. "Or at this hotel." He watched Frank amble over, his bathrobe sagging loosely and opened at the top, exposing his white furry chest.

"He retired a few years ago and has been living here on and off ever since, depending on his marital status back home," Victor said. "He fell in love with Maria."

"Which one?"

"All of them."

Frank greeted the bartender by name, and that was enough for the bartender to know to fix him a fresh passion fruit juice and two fried eggs.

"Comrades," Frank greeted them as he sat on one of the wobbly wooden stools. "Are we set for this evening?"

The three went through the plan again, stopping when the squeaky bartender came by to deliver Frank his juice and eggs.

They would meet Victor's source VZSPARKLEPONY, who was called El Gordo by his friends, on the outskirts of town. It was a delicate meeting, in so many ways. First of all, they were only a short distance from the border with Tamindo, just over which was the heart of FRPT territory. More and more FRPT foot soldiers had been showing up in Kiltoa as of late, but it had become impossible for El Gordo to meet anywhere else. He could always go to Kiltoa from the FRPT base where he lived for family reasons or on a supply run. Meeting anywhere else, even two towns closer to the edge of the jungle, was becoming too risky, raising too many questions for El Gordo to have to find answers to. The meeting would thus be brief, low key, and, Victor hoped, hidden from the prying eyes of any shopkeepers, loiterers, children, or prostitutes who might be on the FRPT's payroll.

That's where Mike and Frank came in. The chief of station back in the capital of Guayita, whom they called Patrón, had insisted on Mike and Frank accompanying Victor. He knew El Gordo was Victor's source, a high-level FRPT militant that Victor had rather easily recruited several weeks ago, but as the meetings became more complex—thanks to the increased FRPT presence in the area—they required more logistics, namely people with guns who could watch Victor's back and make sure he didn't get kidnapped, freeing Victor up to concentrate on El Gordo, his information, and his safety.

Mike was the new deputy chief of Guayita Station, who had recently done a tour in Iraq, and was thus already certified to carry a weapon. Frank knew his way around the Amazon like a jaguar, always watching and ready to strike, but you would never see him unless he wanted you to.

The meeting was risky and Victor knew El Gordo was starting to become scared. He had joined the FRPT years ago, when the organization's leadership followed through on its populist promises, providing schools and health care, food and shelter to Tamindo's poor and underrepresented. He had recalled for Victor rallies in his small hometown, calling on Tamindo's citizens to care for their neighbors and fight for equality, for the rich and poor alike.

He had become disillusioned with the organization over the years, though. While once upon a time he would smuggle medicines into the country to be distributed in Tamindo's poorest regions, increasingly those boxes were filled with precursor chemicals for cocaine. The FRPT had also turned to kidnapping to fund their operations and training. More recently, the group had bombed a hospital. The violence bothered El Gordo, but he had tolerated it when it was aimed at the right cause. When he overheard one of the group's leaders talking about buying guns and ammunition in bulk because of the cost savings, the Marxist magic was gone. He turned CYA informant, giving up FRPT positions and operations, in hopes of preserving and advancing the people's struggle. When Victor gave him his first payment, one thousand American dollars, which arrived in time to pay for his son's emergency appendectomy and which meant his wife could quit one of her jobs, Karl Marx quickly disappeared into the annals of history. He willingly threw in his lot with the capitalists.

The reality of that decision was setting in. El Gordo had agreed to give Victor information on the FRPT, but now that he was in it, living it, and being directed about what kinds of information to get, the gravity of what he was doing and the consequences it entailed had hit him. Victor recognized this phase. Most sources go through it. Victor planned to use tonight's meeting to reassure El Gordo that his decision had been right and he was in good hands.

"Victor, how safe is this? It's like the Wild West out there," Mike said. Victor could hear Mike's voice wavering.

"They haven't kidnapped or killed any foreigners in more than three months," Victor said. "Don't worry."

"Statistically, that's not really in our favor, is it? It means they're due for another kidnapping or killing."

Frank slurped his runny eggs.

"Weren't you in Iraq before this?" Victor asked. "This can't be worse, because Director took away our hazard pay," he said, referring to CYA's headquarters. "According to Washington, Guayandes is safer than Iraq."

"I didn't actually go out in Iraq."

"Didn't go out where?"

"Anywhere. I hardly left my cubicle. It took the first half of my tour to get an ergonomic chair. The second half, I sat in it and adjusted it."

"As long as you can handle a gun and make sure I don't get taken, I'll overlook all that."

"I can handle a gun." He said it as though he were trying to convince himself. "I handled a gun in training. I guess technically I handled a gun today, right? I carried it from the office to the car to here. Yes! I can handle a gun."

"You didn't carry a gun in Iraq?"

"I did. One night. Halloween. It was a huge party. You should have been there. A kegger like I haven't seen in years! And the women, woo!" Mike was animated, until he saw Victor's face. "I went as Indiana Jones," he said, sheepishly. "I carried a plastic gun." He stuttered a bit as he said it.

Victor continued, "We'll each run our SDR then meet at Location Squid. Mike, you'll take the northeast corner. There's a good, dark doorway for you to recon the site before I arrive. Frank, you take southwest."

Frank gave a nearly imperceptible nod. He had been doing this for so long, it would be an evening like any other, running a surveillance detection route through the town's streets and alleys to determine if anyone was following him. Mike did less to inspire confidence. He was repeating Victor's words. "SDR, right. Squid. Got it." When he repeated the word "northeast" he put his hands in front of him and rotated this way and that, thinking hard, trying to figure out which way was northeast. He asked, "Do you have a planned SDR for me?"

"Who has a surveillance detection route planned for them?" Victor asked incredulously. "I gave you a map back in Guayita. Figure out a route to make sure you're not being followed."

"In Iraq, management laid out certain routes officers were allowed to take. Mostly big roads that could accommodate armed personnel carriers. Again, not that I took those routes. My main route was from my condo to the office to the cafeteria to the tennis courts."

"Have you ever recruited a source, Mike?"

"Does a walk-in count?"

"No."

"Then no."

"Other than Iraq, what tours have you done?"

"I worked at the Recruitment Center, helping Director recruit new employees. So I *have* recruited people." Mike gave a stilted laugh.

"Now you're deputy chief of Guayita Station," said Victor, who had six tours plus two war zone trips under his belt. "Cool."

The bartender switched the television to a functioning channel and refilled everyone's glass. Frank was sopping up the rest of his eggs with a piece of toast. A glob of runny yolk had dripped on his bathrobe, which was perilously loose.

"Sovereignty!" a loud voice called from the television. All three CYA men turned to the screen, where Guayandan President Rafa Evorez, El Toro himself, was spouting the populist rhetoric that had made him so popular with the people of Guayandes. "We will not let the swine up north interfere with our sovereignty!" He was speaking indoors and had worked up a sweat. A clump of dark hair was pasted to his broad forehead. He wore a sash with the bright colors of Guayandes' flag, green for the land, blue for the ocean, and red for the blood that had been spilled in the many fights for freedom.

Victor tuned out the droning president and his thoughts turned to Vanessa, who was in the capital city, Guayita, probably knee deep in packing material. He admitted it was bad timing. After weeks of living in a hotel waiting for the embassy to upgrade security at their apartment, he and his family had finally been allowed to move in and have their belongings delivered, on precisely the day he had to go to the jungle for a meeting. Although he also admitted he was glad to be skipping the chaos of the move, and knew Ness was fine with it, even though she would wield it over him ten or twenty years down the line.

Victor had arrived in Guayandes four months ago. Vanessa and their son, Oliver, had arrived two months later, after Oliver had finished the school year in Washington and Vanessa had closed her cases at the FBI, tied up loose ends, and officially gone on leave from the Bureau. He felt a pang of guilt when he thought about it, since she had liked her job and was good at it. She waved it off, eager for an adventure in a new country and confident her skills—and security clearances—would land her a job at the embassy in Guayandes.

Victor recalled picking Ness and Oliver up at Guayita International Airport when they finally arrived after twenty-four hours of traveling. Even though there was a direct flight from Washington operated by Guayandes' national airliner, the CYA had made them take three separate flights with layovers on an American carrier. His six-year-old son had collapsed on the floor of the airport when he saw that his luggage hadn't arrived. Through his tears he had mumbled, "I quit." Victor couldn't blame him. Vanessa and Oliver had spent the next three days wearing the same clothes while they waited for the airline to locate their luggage. The three of them spent the next month living out of a hotel and making the best of it until their house would be ready.

Victor was finding South America to be a rather different experience than Africa and Rubblestan, where he had spent so much time previously. He was happy to take a break from hunting terrorists led by Core Central in Rubblestan. He and Vanessa together had made a small dent a few years back when they had foiled a bomb plot in the United States planned by a West African terrorist Victor had been targeting. While his own leadership at Director cited such successes as proof the United States was winning the Total War On Terror, or TWOT, Victor had watched in frustration as Core Central's various terrorist franchises spread with ease across West and North Africa. He needed a break. When he had seen the listing for the Guayandes position, he looked at a map and noted the total number of Core franchises within a 3,000-mile radius of Guayita was zero. He was in.

Guayandes was also slightly off the beaten path, as far as policy priorities in Washington were concerned. Sure, the country had terrorists, but they weren't the religious kind, nor were they looking to carry out attacks in the United States. They were much more interested in running drugs. Yet, even in that industry, Guayandes was considered secondary. The main focus was on Tamindo, since that was where the FRPT was based. The group's slow spread south into Guayandes was relatively new and, for now at least, not a hot item on Washington's threat matrix. He hoped that meant he could hide a bit from Director's bureaucracy, which had plagued him on other missions.

Victor missed Africa, the sights, and definitely the smells, and the culture. He had spent so much time there, even its corruption was familiar. Victor felt at home in a country whose president proudly visited his Swiss bank account monthly and chartered a private jet for the trip. Living in Guayandes, a socialist country whose president went out of his way to hide his extravagances behind a perverted ideology that claimed to support the people, was novel. Victor was quickly learning, too, that the war on drugs could be as nebulous as the war on terror.

"I am counting on you to support me in the upcoming election. The revolution needs you! I need you! Together we will safeguard our sovereignty! The evil swine will regret that it ever heard of El Toro!" The applause of hundreds of supporters on the television broke Victor's reverie. He looked at the television and saw police holding back the crowds. He wondered how many buses the government had needed to transport all those people in.

Victor took a last swig of coffee. The grounds stuck to the side of the tin mug. He looked at Mike, watching the president and trembling, the case officer who had done a tour in a war zone but could barely handle a gun, who was his immediate boss but had never met or recruited a source. He looked at Frank, who had turned to gaze at the four Marias in this hotel that—after a career spent hopscotching the world, leaving broken marriages behind him—was the closest thing he had to a home. His bathrobe was all but slipping off. His hair was a mess. Victor thought of his wife, who was probably cursing in Spanish at the movers right now but who had sent him off to the jungle with a kiss. He thought of Patrón and the other officers, his friends, back in Guayita Station, working their angles on the same objective he was.

This was Victor Caro's team. The team who would help destroy a major revolutionary group that was responsible for years of war and bloodshed in Latin America and on the streets of the United States. The team who would cover him as he operated in a country whose president was intent on sticking it to the United States any way he could. The team that he would rely on to meet a frightened source in the middle of a remote town that perfectly marked the nexus between terrorism and narco-trafficking, where he could easily get kidnapped and whisked away to a jungle prison where he could only imagine some TV anchor reminding viewers each night that CYA case officer Victor Caro had now been held captive for forty-four days.

He smiled. Sometimes, nothing was better than life in the CYA.

CHAPTER TWO

"Why the fuck are you doing this?" Vanessa stared at herself in the mirror. She tried to smile. It looked fake. She rolled her eyes, touched up her lipstick, and took a deep breath. As an FBI special agent, she had interviewed cold-hearted murderers, convicted terrorists, and a man who had eaten someone else's brain. Yet she did not feel prepared for the challenge she was about to face. She had agreed to attend Lunch Bunch.

Lunch Bunch was an occasional event organized by the spouses of embassy employees, an opportunity for "dependents"—as employee family members were called in the US government's progressive lingo—to get to know each other and mingle and thus, hopefully, not feel useless. A dependent who felt useless or agitated could become a problem for the employee and, by extension, for the US government. It was best for all parties if everyone was kept entertained.

Becoming a dependent hadn't been Vanessa's plan, in fact. She had spent the last few years methodically working her way up the FBI's ladder in Washington, while Victor did stints at CYA's headquarters, called Director, and in the field. The arrangement wasn't always perfect, but still, they had married and had a child and made it work, despite sometimes living radically different lives.

Once, shortly after Oliver was born, Victor had called Vanessa from Rubblestan, where he had gone to chase terrorists for several months. As Vanessa recounted her day changing diapers and taking their newborn for a stroll in the park, she heard explosions on the other end of the phone.

"Victor, what's happening?"

"Some militants from Core Central are lobbing mortars at the base," he said. "Don't worry. They don't know how to aim."

She had stared at the infant in her lap, unable to reconcile that two such contrary realities could exist at once: her baby sleeping peacefully and her husband being shot at by terrorists.

Their marriage survived the stress that came with Vanessa being a new and single parent while working full-time and worrying about her husband, and with Victor coping with seeing war. After Rubblestan, he returned to Director but did a few temporary stints out in the field, mostly in Africa, to get an occasional adrenaline rush.

When the opening in Guayita came up, both Victor and Vanessa had been eager to jump. It was an adventure they could all have together. By sheer luck, the FBI had a position opening in Guayita at the same time as Victor's assignment. Ness worked her contacts at Bureau headquarters and secured the job. She spent a year preparing and learning Spanish. Six months before she was scheduled to leave, the Bureau pulled the position out of Guayandes and put it in Tamindo. When she inquired about why, the human resources officer had said, "If you were ready to go to Guayandes, you should be ready to go to Tamindo. It's basically the same country, just next door. You will have to reapply, though."

"You had already offered me the position when it was in Guayandes," Vanessa had said.

"This is a new position. It's in Tamindo."

"But it is exactly the same job."

"Except it is in Tamindo, so you have to reapply. You should do so quickly. Several people have already expressed an interest. Also, we won't be filling it until next year."

"Why next year?"

"Can you imagine the havoc we would wreak if we asked employees to move on a moment's notice?"

Victor and Vanessa had opened a nice bottle of wine to discuss their choices. In the end, she was the driving factor. She was tired of the programmed life of parents in Washington—play dates, soccer, birthday parties every Saturday. She felt numb in the routine. When a neighbor had stopped by to share her excitement about the new lower price on kale smoothies at the local Whole Foods, Vanessa had thrown a Starbucks coffee mug at the wall and watched it shatter, just to feel something.

She was also tired of a desk job and missed the fun of being in the field. To return to the field, she would have to apply for a position she had already been offered but that had been transferred to another country and would not be filled for another year, if they honored it the second time around. They could pull the position again. Victor, on the other hand, had a secure offer overseas.

The lure of a new country, the boundless opportunities to discover everything new, was too much for Vanessa. She didn't love her job enough to give up the chance to go to Guayandes. Plus, after all the separations imposed on them by their jobs, they were ready, all three of them, to be together as a family. They were ready for an adventure they could all have together.

Still, Vanessa didn't know if she was ready for Lunch Bunch. She looked around the apartment. The moving boxes were gone, but so much of their life remained scattered about. She remembered something her grandmother had always said about messes: "The good news is, it will be still be there when you come back, so you can do it later." Her grandmother was right. She could do it later.

She headed out the door.

Ellie was waiting for her in a huge, nine-person minivan.

"I don't know why the fuck I'm doing this," Vanessa said to Ellie, as she climbed into the front seat. She could hear "The Little Mermaid" playing on the DVD player in the back of the van.

"We're going to play nice and make new friends," Ellie said. The tires screeched as she peeled out. A crushed juice box that had been sitting on the armrest between them fell to the floor. Vanessa looked out across the valley below them as the car climbed a steep hill out of the housing compound where Victor, Vanessa, and Oliver now lived. A large cloud hovered above the valley, like a spaceship preparing to suck up a mass of urban specimens. Below it, Vanessa could see the city, a maze of squat square buildings. Above it, on the far side of the valley, she saw Paxico volcano, covered in snow even though it was summer.

Ellie waved enthusiastically at the three guards who manned the security gate at the entrance to Vanessa's housing complex. "Bye, Jorge!" she yelled through her rolled-down window.

"You know the names of the guards at my gate?" Vanessa asked. "I don't know their names yet."

"I figure at least one of them is named Jorge. They smiled, so I was probably right."

Vanessa pressed her lips together and suppressed a laugh. She had met Ellie Sands shortly after they had both arrived in Guayita, in a side room at the embassy where new arrivals often decamped to take a break from the insanity involved in getting moved in and settled in a new place. Vanessa had gone to take a breather after the people in shipping had informed her that, while it was true they had told her the previous day that her shipment was on its way, they now realized it had been held up in Miami by a hurricane and likely would not arrive for another month. And while yes, Victor and Vanessa's car had arrived two weeks earlier, Guayandan customs officials had implemented a new regulation that required all cars coming from the United States to be held for three weeks, at which point an additional import tariff must be paid. This was apparently because a US Embassy political officer had been five minutes late to a meeting at the Guayandan Foreign Ministry and the foreign minister was so offended he had decided to punish the embassy as a whole. The government of the United States had had to launch an official complaint with the Guayandan Foreign Ministry. Victor and Vanessa's car was now a hostage of a diplomatic spat caused by a traffic jam.

Ellie had retreated to the side room as well, after prying her new house keys from the housing manager. He had told her she would have to wait another six weeks before moving in, so that the embassy could install no-slip grips on the house's wooden steps, a new housing regulation implemented after a diplomat in Mongolia slipped while wearing fuzzy slippers and had to be medically evacuated to Beijing for a broken foot. Ellie had been living with her husband and three children in a hotel for a month. So she was rather pleased that when the housing manager informed her about the new regulation, her middle child began kicking the man's desk. The noise made the baby she was holding cry. She promptly handed the baby to the housing manager and called out to her eldest daughter to come help with the middle child, who was now also singing loudly. "Do you want us to leave?" Ellie asked over the chaos. "That's how the hotel feels, too."

She had the keys to her new home within the hour and Vanessa realized she could learn from this woman. Ellie had the added qualities of being optimistic and funny. Her husband, Simon, worked in the same office as Victor, and their eldest daughter, Heidi, was the same age as Oliver and would be in the same class at school. Vanessa and Ellie became fast friends, two CYA spouses, two dependents, who were now on their way to attend Lunch Bunch.

"I'm not real good at playing nice," Vanessa said over the sound of a singing shrimp coming from the DVD player in the back. She looked at the back seat to confirm there were no children.

They drove past the residence of President Rafa Evorez. While the Presidential Palace was located downtown in the heart of the city, the president's private home was here, a mere block from Victor and Vanessa's house. By Guayandan standards, his house was sprawling. A three-car garage, two completed stories, and a fully intact roof. Other buildings nearby were cinderblock rectangles with flat roofs with steel poles sticking out the top. The neighborhood had never really taken off. With the exception of two police motorcycles out front, no one would know the president and his family lived there.

Ellie swerved around a pothole and turned down a dirt road and up an alley to arrive at a different housing compound. As she approached the security checkpoint, she barely slowed down and smiled and waved at the guards, "Hi, Jorge!" The gate opened and the guards waved back and ushered the minivan through.

"Do you know these guards?" Vanessa asked.

"No."

They parked in front of a large wall with glass shards sticking out like razor blades cemented to the top, ready to slice any intruder who dared to climb the wall or any pigeon unfortunate enough to land there. Cars lined both sides of the small road, mostly American-made SUVs. One had a George W. Bush sticker on it.

"Do you know which house?" Vanessa asked when she saw multiple buzzers outside the heavy gate. This was a housing compound within the bigger housing compound. Vanessa was beginning to realize Guayita had a lot of compounds. Most living was done behind huge walls.

"No," Ellie said, as she pushed each button, one after the other. Various voices sprang from the little speaker, all speaking Spanish and asking who was ringing. Ellie responded with a simple and perky, "Oh, sorry!" in English and kept pushing buttons until the gate clicked open.

They walked through and saw a giant expanse of green grass with five houses, each enormous with its own SUV parked in the driveway. With the exception of security bars on every window, Vanessa thought it looked like any suburb in Northern Virginia. She shivered.

The front door of the middle house opened and a young blond woman welcomed them in. "Hellooooo!" she nearly screamed in a high-pitched voice. "Come in!" She drew out the word "in" for about five seconds. "I'm Savannah!" Again, she drew out the sound for several seconds. She was wearing a sequined top in the middle of the day.

Vanessa looked toward Ellie, as if to ask, "Is this normal?" but Ellie walked with confidence to the door and hugged Savannah while releasing her own, "Eeeeeee! Thanks for having us!" She smiled back at Vanessa, urging her with her eyes to take a chance and enter.

Inside were more high-pitched squeaks of hello and hugs and kisses all around. On the dining table, Vanessa saw a spread of food and was shocked, not for how different it was, but how familiar: Doritos, Tostitos, Old El Paso salsa, and jarred guacamole lined the table, along with bottles of Pepsi and a carton of Newman's Own Lemonade. Avocados were a main staple in Guayandes. Vanessa found the jarred guacamole particularly curious.

"I went to the commissary this morning!" Savannah said, referring to the small grocery store at the embassy that sold products from the United States. Savannah clapped her hands together. She seemed to glow. "I bought us great snacks!" Savannah was enthusiastic about everything, it seemed.

"My napkin shipment from Target just arrived!" said another woman. "Just in time!" She began laying out the bright yellow-and-blue-striped napkins in an elaborate display on a side table, paying very close attention to her work, lining up edges and then pulling back to view her handiwork from afar.

"I brought Oreos!" shouted another.

A Guayandan woman, Savannah's housekeeper Vanessa guessed, entered carrying a large silver platter with a silver dome covering its contents. She placed it on the table and removed the dome with a flourish to reveal a stack of empanadas. At least Guayandes had one representative in this commissary-concocted cornucopia.

Vanessa found herself moving closer to Ellie, like a child staying close to its mother when the surroundings are too confusing. Her head was spinning. She was in a foreign country, but this table looked like America had just vomited.

Vanessa grabbed a glass of wine while Savannah urged everyone to "Sit! Sit!" and motioned to her housekeeper to serve food around the room. "Sit, Vanessa!" she said as she put both hands on Vanessa's shoulders and gently pushed her into a plush chair. Half a dozen other women found seats around the living room as a big bowl of chips circled through the group. "Everyone, this is Vanessa! This is Ellie! Their husbands work at the embassy! This is their first Lunch Bunch! Let's make them feel welcome!"

Vanessa looked around at six enthusiastic and bright-eyed faces staring back at her as they each let forth a friendly greeting and bombardment of questions.

"When did you arrive?"

"Is this your first post?"

"Has your stuff arrived?"

"Do you have housing yet?"

"How many kids do you have? Which school will he go to?"

Vanessa was not used to being on this side of the questioning and preferred to gulp her wine and let Ellie answer, which she was happy to do.

"Ladies, stop!" Savannah yelled in fake admonishment. "Why don't we go around the room and introduce ourselves? I think that will be easier. I'll start. I'm Savannah Harris! This is my home! We've been here two years. Our sons, Brayden and Brennan, are two and four. They love Bob the Builder and Clifford, even though in real life Brennan is allergic to dogs. My husband is a former Marine but is now a civilian in the Defense Attaché's office and is a GS-14, but should be promoted to fifteen this summer! Christie? You go next."

A very pregnant woman sat up. "I'm Christie Quaid. My husband is with the Drug Enforcement Administration. He's a GS-14 also. We've technically been in Guayita for almost three years, but I've only spent six months here because this is my third pregnancy and for each one I go back to the US for six or seven, sometimes eight months. Today," she paused for dramatic effect, as she gave an open-mouthed smile to the room, "little Samuel sat on his training pot and peed!"

The ladies applauded and let out various sounds of "Awwww!" and "Congratulations!"

They continued around the room, describing their husbands' job and grade level and counting their children. They arrived at Vanessa.

She took another gulp of wine then faced the eyes focused intently on her. "I'm Vanessa. I'm an FBI agent. GS-14, not that that's really anyone's business."

"You mean your husband is FBI," Christie said.

"No," Vanessa said. "I am."

"What does your husband do?"

"He pushes paper at the embassy."

"What grade level is he?"

"I have no idea." The women looked confused. Vanessa pushed on, "As I said, my background is as an FBI agent. I took a leave of absence but I figure with my background there must be something at the embassy I can do."

"Oh, there's plenty to do!" said Savannah.

"Do you knit, Vanessa? You *have* to join the knitting club!"

"Who's coming to my scrapbooking event this weekend? I've got new decorative tape and will teach some tricks about using feathers to brighten the page."

"Are we doing Bunko this Friday?"

"Who wants to come get Botox with me tomorrow?"

Vanessa tossed back the rest of her wine. She recalled interviewing an inmate in Colorado's Supermax prison, his hands shackled to his waist, his ankles in chains. He was over six feet tall and was serving a life sentence for beheading his three sisters because he thought they had been sent by God to embarrass him. He had leaned over to Vanessa and whispered, "Those were three easy slices."

Yet when she looked around her now, Savannah in her sequined top, Christie weighing the pros and cons of a combined C-section/tummy tuck, all these women bearing food from the embassy's own minimart, she had never felt so out of place. She wanted to go home.

CHAPTER THREE

In his tiny hotel room in the jungle, Victor went through his checklist and agenda for his meeting with El Gordo one last time. Mike and Frank had left the hotel already, taking different routes to their respective positions, where they would be tasked with keeping Victor safe. That way, Victor could focus on his asset.

He grabbed his Glock from the bed, checked it one last time, and tucked it into its holster, before donning a brown leather vest. He looked in the mirror. Vanessa's mother had given him the vest. He never would have chosen it on his own; it looked like Indiana Jones had joined The Village People. But Victor liked the ample cut of the vest, which easily concealed his Glock, and its many pockets, which could hold ammunition.

He reached for his cigarettes. The pack was empty. He'd buy another on the way; an extra stop was actually a good idea, another opportunity to see if he was being followed. He left the hotel on foot.

He wound through the streets and markets, watching every face, every car, every mule cart, to see if he saw anyone twice. He rounded a corner and entered a small shop. He asked the shopkeeper for a pack of cigarettes.

The shopkeeper placed the pack on the counter. "One hundred fifty chavis."

Damn, trafficked cigarettes are cheap, Victor thought. That was about one dollar and fifty cents. He handed the man a five-hundred chavi bill. The shopkeeper set it down and rummaged through his cash drawer.

"Do you have anything smaller?"

Victor did not have anything smaller—he *did* have one thousand dollars in cash in one of his leather vest pockets—but he could see that the man, in fact, did have change. He pointed to the drawer. "There's three fifty right there."

"If I give you that, I won't have any change for the next customer."

"You won't sell me the cigarettes?" Victor asked.

"What if someone comes in and wants to buy something, and I don't have change? Then he won't buy it."

"*I* came in and want to buy something."

"Do you have change?"

Victor took back his five hundred chavis. He needed clarity as he approached his meeting with El Gordo. This conversation wasn't helping.

He went back outside. The sun was down and the streets were emptying. A woman swept her storefront stairs while a child pushed a tricycle through the dirt nearby. Victor approached the meeting site, a poorly lit dirt alley. He saw Frank, tucked away in the shadows. Victor glanced at the northeast corner where Mike was supposed to be covering him. The doorway was empty. Mike was a no-show. Victor's left flank was exposed.

Victor had less than one second, one footstep, to make a decision: turn down the alley and meet his asset, trusting that Frank alone could secure the site and prevent either Victor or El Gordo from spending the next twenty years as a guest in an FRPT prison camp, or abort, returning to Guayita with nothing and having to wait several more weeks for another opportunity to talk to El Gordo. His heart beat in his throat. Turn and take the risk, or abort a meeting he had spent weeks planning for and face the disappointment of the lost opportunity? Turn? Abort? He took a deep breath.

He turned down the alley.

As he stepped toward the side, in the shadow of a wall, El Gordo arrived from the opposite direction. Victor's internal stopwatch started. They had about two minutes; any longer and the risk was too great.

"*Amigo*," El Gordo said. "It is no longer safe here. Kiltoa. Guayandes. They are coming."

"Who is coming?" asked Victor.

"FRPT. They are crossing the border daily now. They've set up camps on this side. The army of Tamindo is securing Tamindo, but it can't take apart the FRPT. Even Reis now spends most of his time here, in Guayandes."

"Paulo Reis? The leader of the FRPT?"

"He wants an operational center on this side of the border. Your Congress gave money to President Pulu to secure Tamindo from the FRPT, but as long as there is demand for cocaine in the United States, the supply will find a way. Some of that demand is from your Congress." El Gordo laughed.

Victor heard a chirp. It was Frank, signaling him the meeting needed to be over. Victor slipped El Gordo the envelope with one thousand dollars, and they each continued in their own direction.

Victor started on his route back toward the hotel. Mike had left him vulnerable in the middle of a jungle town that was quickly becoming an FRPT stronghold. The threat of kidnapping was real. El Gordo's information that the FRPT's leader was traveling to Guayandes regularly had driven the point home. Victor had brought Mike and Frank to be his team for a reason. How could Mike have left him and Frank out there?

He found Mike waiting for him at the hotel bar, a bottle of tequila and three shot glasses standing at attention. Mike looked like he had just vomited, which, in fact, he had.

Victor crossed the lobby slowly, Mike seeming to twitch with each step and growing paler as Victor got closer. He took a deep breath, sat up straight, and composed himself, picking up the bottle to pour three solid-sized shots. He knocked one back, set the glass back on the table, then said to Victor, "I can explain."

Victor drank a shot and sat down, waiting for an explanation he knew would never placate him.

"I, I," Mike started with a stutter. "You see, the map," he paused. "It was dark, and I, uh, well, you see, I got turned around. I think maybe I should have turned left instead of right at that bodega." He continued rambling, as though trying to explain to himself where exactly he had gotten lost in this small shit of a town that was laid out in a grid. Victor tuned him out and took another shot, returning to the present as Mike said, "I'm just happy I made it back to the hotel alive!"

Frank entered the lobby and crossed to them quickly. He took a shot, still standing, and looked at Victor. "What the fuck happened to him?" He gestured toward Mike with a slight nod of his head.

"He got lost," Victor said, pouring new shots for Frank and himself, placing the bottle back on the table without filling Mike's glass.

"Does he know the town's a fucking grid?"

Victor shrugged and pushed himself out of his seat. He grabbed the tequila bottle and his glass in one hand and gave a small wave to the others before retreating to his room. He flopped on the bed and looked at the bottle and shot glass. He tossed the shot glass aside and took a big swig straight from the bottle.

He went over the meeting with El Gordo in his head. The president of Tamindo had managed to clear his ranks of corruption and restore some law and order on his side of the border. The problem was that the FRPT was not dismantled at all. Its operational territory in Tamindo was being stripped away, but the strategy was proving only to push the group over to the Guayandan side of the border.

That Reis himself was risking the border crossing—regularly, according to El Gordo—meant the group felt safe enough in Guayandes. The leader of South America's strongest revolutionary group, who was building it into a major drug trafficking organization, felt safe in Guayandes. Why? Was the Guayandan military incapable of stopping the FRPT from entering their territory? Or were they turning a blind eye? Did Guayandan President Evorez know? Was the government of Guayandes sanctioning FRPT operations in Guayandan territory?

Victor took another sip of tequila. He could hear Frank and one of the Marias down the hall. On the other side of the wall, he heard Mike talking to himself.

"You can do this, man. Come on. Put up your hands!"

Victor heard metal clicking sounds. He realized Mike was taking apart and putting together his gun. He pictured him next door, checking in the mirror to see if his expression was menacing enough, working on his stance, the gun pointed at the wall he shared with Victor's room. Victor grabbed a pillow and moved to the floor, trying to block from his mind the fact that Mike, the deputy chief of station and therefore his boss, had left him exposed in a narco-terror paradise and was, at that very moment, pointing a gun at him through a wall. It might make for two very long years in Guayandes. More if he got caught or kidnapped. Less if he got shot.

Victor could hear Mike flicking the gun around. At one point, he dropped it. "The name's Quinn. Mike Quinn."

Victor pulled the pillow over his ears and drifted off to sleep.

CHAPTER FOUR

Guayandan President Rafa Evorez, also known as El Toro, was plopped in his comfy chair behind his enormous desk, which was empty except for a single piece of paper and a bronze statue of a condor alighting from a branch. He was dressed in a green, blue, and red nylon sweat suit, the colors of the Guayandan flag. His closest adviser, Segundo Espina, stood in front of El Toro's desk, his hands clutched behind his back, an impatient look on his face. Evorez was tugging at his jacket zipper, trying to close the jacket over his extending belly.

"My President," Segundo said, trying to get Evorez to pay attention. "Word has arrived from my contacts at Guayandes Petroleum that the workers are," he paused a moment before continuing, "not fully embracing your vision for revolution."

Evorez tugged at his T-shirt, which had gotten stuck in the zipper.

"As my wise leader knows, Guayandes Petroleum is Guayandes' largest company. Its image as a symbol of Guayandes' economic prowess and, therefore, your influential leadership cannot be overstated. The workers have vowed to strike."

The T-shirt ripped out of the zipper, and Evorez pulled it up too quickly, catching a piece of skin on his neck. He let out a *gah!*

Segundo continued, his voice louder, "Their subversion, *Señor Presidente*, is an affront to the revolution, and you are the embodiment of the revolution."

Evorez dabbed a tissue on his bleeding neck.

"El Toro, their counter-revolutionary behavior is an affront to *you*!"

Evorez finally looked up. "They don't like me?"

"They are mocking your socialist committees. They are mocking the revolution. They are mocking you! You must solidify your position before the election."

"That is unacceptable!" Evorez banged his fist on the table. "Why should I have to have an election?"

"*Señor Presidente*, your opposition is cowardly in your shadow, but still, you must show the people the leader you are."

"Will I win?"

"I can assure you, you will, but this is the moment to appear strong, to *be* strong."

Segundo waited for Evorez to say something. Evorez looked at him.

"Do you have any ideas?" Evorez asked.

"It's time to be bold, to show them who is in charge. Anyone suspected of plotting against the revolution should be fired!"

"That sounds reasonable," Evorez said.

He picked up a pen and, emboldened by his adviser's words, signed the order Segundo had placed in front of him. Any employee of the state-run petroleum company who did not adequately support the revolution was now terminated. He handed the paper to Segundo, who brandished it above his head and yelled, "*¡Por la lucha!*"

"Yes! For the struggle! How many people did I fire?"

"Nearly twenty thousand, sir."

Evorez looked anxious. "That's nearly half of the employees. How," he stammered. "How will the company function?"

"The forces of history are on your side! Your Excellency, your vision will lead us."

"You're probably right."

"You could, of course, offer those jobs to some of your supporters who are looking to serve you but have thus far been unable to acquire full-time employment. You will be creating jobs and lowering unemployment, while advancing the revolution."

"Good idea."

"Sir, I have also heard of rumblings in the ranks of the federal police."

"Do I need to fire them, too?"

"I'll handle them, El Toro. But please, be careful who you trust."

"I give you my fullest confidence, Segundo."

"Very good, Your Excellency. Very good."

CHAPTER FIVE

B it by bit, Victor and Mike's SUV ascended in altitude until the road was a single, suicidal lane with a sheer drop of hundreds of feet to the canyon below. It was raining, decreasing visibility and making the road slippery and more of a death trap than usual. Victor popped chocolate-covered coffee beans in his mouth as he drove, enjoying the fact that Mike looked frozen in the passenger seat, his eyes fixed wide and straight ahead, his white knuckles locked around the passenger-side handle. He was still angry that Mike had left him vulnerable in the middle of FRPT territory the night before.

"What brought you to South America, Mike? I mean, a war zone tour but Director still saw fit to send you to this shithole?" Victor asked, chewing on another coffee bean.

"It was one of the few openings at my grade level. Director said it would help me get my next promotion."

Mike let out a "Whoa!" while Victor careened around another corner and narrowly missed a cow that was standing on the side of the road chewing grass. It didn't flinch, chewing slowly as it watched the SUV speed by.

They continued on mostly in silence, Mike gasping every now and then when a bus as wide as the road came around a curve and sandwiched their car against the mountain, or when Victor took a hairpin turn at full speed, still smiling and enjoying the ride. The closer they got to the capital, the wider the roads became, although their lethality remained firmly intact thanks to the many pickup trucks with loose materials thrown in the back that would fly out once the truck reached a certain speed. Every now and then, Victor would dodge a flying piece of tin, part of a broken wooden chair, or a large but defunct washing machine.

As Victor swerved around an empty chicken coop, he saw a giant pile of dirt ahead, dark, wet, and high, taller than the SUV they were in. The rains had caused a landslide, the side of the mountain sliding onto the highway and blocking all the lanes, leaving only a small passage along a cliff to get by. Victor switched into four-wheel drive and plowed over a portion of the dirt, Mike staring at the drop below and holding his breath. They bumped up and down, slipping over the mud.

"You ever miss Iraq?" Victor asked. Mike didn't respond except to make a sound like he was suffocating.

They emerged on the other side, unscathed but with an even muddier car than before. Victor slammed the brakes. "Is that a roadblock down there?" He grabbed a set of binoculars and peered farther down the road. He saw a row of military trucks and a tank. "It's a military roadblock."

He pulled out his cell phone. No signal. They were still too far out of Guayita to get reception. "Yours work?" he asked Mike, who shook his head no while he fiddled with his phone.

Victor double-checked that the car was in four-wheel drive and slammed it into reverse.

***

Vanessa stood in the middle of her new living room and took a deep breath. Done. She had stayed up most of the night, but she had managed to put everything in its new place. For the first time in months, her family had a place to call home, if only for the next two years. Because Guayita was a "furnished post" in government-speak, the embassy provided most of the furniture. In this case, the embassy had provided a palette of pastels, like a flamingo pink-and-green couch offset by teal and ivory couch pillows.

Oliver was at school, finally falling into a first-grade routine, after weeks of commuting to school in a taxi from a hotel. He had missed several days early on when a stomach virus landed him in the emergency room, a common occurrence for new arrivals as they adjusted to being exposed to new germs and bacteria in the food. Oliver had probably sipped water directly from the faucet, forgetting for a moment his parents' instructions only to drink bottled water. Once that had passed, he got a few good days in at school before President Evorez shut it down. The private American school, unbeknown to Evorez, had opened two weeks before the Guayandan public schools were scheduled to begin. When the president returned from vacation and saw the American school open, he concluded it was a ruse by the Americans and the Guayandan elite—who were wealthy enough to send their children to private school and therefore must be in cahoots with the Americans—to keep the ordinary young citizens of Guayandes less educated. The elites were trying to get two extra weeks of education in order to remain elite and keep everyone else down. By presidential decree, El Toro shut down the American school for two weeks, thus leveling the playing field for all students in Guayandes.

At long last Vanessa and Victor's car had been released from customs car prison and was waiting for her at a garage downtown. A local Guayandan worker at the embassy had called her that morning to tell her the good news. When Vanessa had asked what papers she needed to prove it was her car, the Guayandan said nothing, but Vanessa could almost hear his noncommittal shrug over the phone. When she had asked about license plates, he had told her to come to the embassy after she had the car, and he would give her a photocopy of a license plate to tape on the rear window.

"To tape on the window?" Vanessa asked.

"Yes, like Scotch tape. Until your real license plates arrive."

"How long does that take?"

"Usually about two years."

Vanessa took a taxi to the customs parking lot, convinced they would never allow her to leave with her car, since she had no papers proving it was hers. She arrived at the lot and saw her new gray Xterra sitting there, a half-asleep guard leaning on the fence outside a gatehouse where Vanessa could see a lot of keys. She decided to take an Ellie approach: she smiled and waved and said hello in Spanish very brightly. She almost called him Jorge, just to see, but decided against it. He smiled back and entered the gatehouse, asking simply, "Xterra?"

He handed Vanessa the key and opened the gate. She wondered if she were to come back tomorrow, would he let her take a second car? Maybe even a third? Instead of Lunch Bunch, they should all see how many cars they could drive off a customs lot with.

She climbed into her new car, which she had bought in Washington shortly before leaving. It had seemed so big there, parked next to a Smart car. But here, where the roads were jammed with armored Pajeros and Patrols, driven by the bodyguards of the wealthy, it looked rather normal. It had only fifty-nine miles on it, the distance from the dealership to the shipping container that had carried it south and through the Panama Canal. Someone from the shipping company had met her at the dealership and driven her car away for her. She realized that, with the exception of the test drive, she had never driven this car and was now about to be let loose to drive in the chaos of Guayita.

The gate opened and she approached the street, avoiding a stray dog on the left side of the gate and a toddler who had wandered a few steps away from his mother who was selling Fanta in plastic bags off an overturned box on the right side of the gate. She pulled into traffic and was immediately immersed in the bedlam. Three lanes of cars in a space meant only for two, the brown exhaust of the bus in front pooling around Vanessa's car, frail men selling plastic chachkas and rainbow Slinkys, children in dirty clothes begging. She pushed her way into the turn lane, knowing she had to go north and hoping this road would take her there. While she was waiting for the light to turn, a man selling an airbrushed Last Supper painting in a heavy embellished frame stood in front of her car. Jesus wore neon blue robes and his orange halo made his head look like it was on fire. She considered it—it would certainly always remind her of Guayita—but decided against it.

The light turned green and a woman selling mandarins approached. Now, this was actually useful, Vanessa thought. As the line of cars behind her extended and honked with impatience, she sifted through her purse for a hundred chavis, which she handed to the woman, pleased with her first off-the-street purchase, completed precisely when the light turned red. She waited, tempted again by someone selling sunglasses—"Real Gucci!" he insisted—and another selling a hammock.

She made it through the intersection and headed north, swerving around cars that stopped in the middle of the street. One car came to a halt in the far left lane. A frail older lady in a bright indigenous dress got out. She hunched so badly, it was though she were doubled over, her blue shawl curling up by her neck from gravity. She shuffled across two lanes of traffic, without a glance at the approaching cars, making her way earnestly to the broken sidewalk where a stray dog sniffed her.

As Vanessa continued north, she could see traffic building up ahead and she decided to find a way around. She turned into an alley, down another road, and rounded a corner where she found herself in a lane meant only for city buses. Standing in the lane, a few feet ahead of her, was a policeman.

"Shit," she said. He stood directly in front of her car, giving her no choice but to stop. He stepped around and knocked on her window, a look of bemusement on his face as he tapped his baton in his open palm.

"This lane is reserved for buses, *señora*, and this," he tapped the top of the car with his baton, "is not a bus."

Vanessa assessed her position. She had no papers proving the car was hers, no proof of insurance, no license plate. She did have—*thank god!* she thought—the best get-out-of-jail-free card that exists: a diplomatic ID from the Guayandan Foreign Ministry. The flimsy yellow card, inexpertly laminated, granted her diplomatic immunity. She smiled politely at the police officer and, although she spoke Spanish quite well, said in broken Spanish that she was lost. "*Por favor*, Mr. Officer, could you direct me?" Her appeal to his chivalry seemed to soften him. He put the baton back in its holster and gave her a warm look.

"You need to exit this lane. Up there." He pointed to where she could get out of the median-encased bus lane. "Be sure to go around Amazonas," he said, referring to one of the main avenues in Guayita. "There's a demonstration, federal police, and you don't want to drive into a crowd of federal police. I still have to give you a ticket. Where is your license plate?"

"I am on my way to get it now," Vanessa said.

"You are not allowed to drive without a license plate."

"Which is why I am on my way now to get it from the American embassy."

"Ah! You are from the embassy? You won't have a license plate for a long time! If you'd like, I can expedite the payment of your citation. You can pay me directly and your ticket will be taken care of."

Vanessa was so thrilled to be presented with her first bribe in Guayandes, she almost felt bad, realizing she should be angry instead. "I'm afraid I can't pay you directly. Why don't you give me your name and badge number, and I will be sure the embassy informs your superior officer when my citation is paid, so your boss knows what fine work you've done."

He became less warm, but was that a hint of admiration in his eyes? Vanessa wondered.

"Listen, since I have you here," he said after a moment, "my sister needs a visa. Do you think you can help?"

The game was no longer amusing, just tiring. She had made a mistake, to be sure, by ending up in the bus lane, but that hardly merited two bribe attempts. "I'm afraid I don't have any contacts who deal with visas," she said. "I'm here on a special assignment, working with your government to combat police corruption. I'm sure you would agree, it's a rather big problem in Guayandes." She looked at him patiently, a smile on her face. He stared back a moment, nodded, and stepped back from the car, an arm extended, allowing her to go.

She drove on, down another road in order to avoid the demonstration the police officer had told her about, and was at another light trying to figure out what fruit a woman was trying to sell her when Vanessa's cell phone rang. It was Ellie.

"Are you OK? Where are you?" Ellie asked urgently.

"I just picked up my car. What's up?"

"It's a coup! You have to get off the streets. I'm going to get my kids from the school now. I can get Oliver, too."

"Wait, what? A coup?" Vanessa looked around her. The woman selling, what was that fruit? Two people in work uniforms crossing the street. A dirty, long-haired juggler on a unicycle doing tricks while his younger brother went car to car asking for money. Everything looked normal to her.

"There was a demonstration. The police or something. They shot President Evorez! He's alive, but they're sending out the military."

"Everything is calm where I am. I'm not too far from the school, but call me when you get there and I'll let you know how far out I am." She was about to pull into the intersection when a tank rolled by. The juggler continued throwing balls in the air. A camouflaged armored personnel carrier passed by next. Then she heard gunshots.

She tore out of the intersection, turning through the unfamiliar streets in an unfamiliar—and very big—car, remembering that it weighed a ton and could be used as a weapon if need be. Other than the tank, the APC, and a gunshot in the distance every now and then, though, the streets were normal. Traffic moved normally. No one looked panicked. Everything continued like usual. Vanessa had always figured a coup would be more, what? What did she think? More terrorizing? More chaotic? More energetic? Well, at least she had thought a coup would be more noticeable.

Vanessa wondered why the police were demonstrating, although she figured it likely had to do with delayed salaries. Evorez had only recently fired nearly half the employees at Guayandes Petroleum, after they had organized to demand their back pay. Evorez had read it as a sign they were taking a counter-revolutionary stance and sacked them. The president couldn't recognize he had mismanaged the country's funds for years. Almost no one paid taxes because it was cheaper to pay bribes. Yet Evorez had made many promises to build housing and schools and hospitals for the rural areas in order to maintain his popularity. It left him no money to pay his own workers, including the police. It wasn't sustainable.

Vanessa pulled up to the school as Ellie rang her again.

"I'm here," Vanessa said. "I'll be inside in a minute." She jumped down from her car and made her way impatiently through the school's security checkpoint, a small guardhouse overflowing with nervous parents anxious to retrieve their children and shut them inside their barred-windowed homes behind electric-fenced walls inside guarded compounds. Shit could go south quickly in a place like this, Vanessa realized, and felt her own urge to get her child safely behind walls.

She ran across the school's well-manicured campus. Several parakeets tweeted in a large, ornate cage outside a group of classrooms. A llama meandered the grounds. Oliver sat outside his classroom with the rest of his class, kids fooling around and laughing like kids, blissfully unaware of the danger lurking down the street, where the military and the police from the same country were lining up against each other. Evorez was not the most stable leader in the best of times. Vanessa worried what he might do when threatened.

"No school!" Oliver yelled joyfully to his mother when he saw her. His friends laughed and celebrated with him. Ellie was there with Heidi.

"With the stomach bug absences, Evorez's closing of the school for two weeks, and now this coup, it will be a miracle if Oliver finishes first grade in Guayita," Vanessa said to Ellie.

"Guayandes is like its volcanoes, Ness. Sometimes it explodes. That's what Jorge told me."

"Who?"

"My gardener."

"Is his name really Jorge?"

"He answers when I call him that."

"Does he speak English? Because you don't speak Spanish."

"He understands me."

They hugged each other goodbye and Vanessa left with Oliver.

"Can I have a snack? Can we go to the park? Can Max come over to play? Can we go swimming? Can I eat? Can I eat now? Oh, look! A penny!" he leaned down to pick up a penny off the sidewalk. Oh, it was good to be six years old, Vanessa thought.

They made their way back to their house, Oliver opening and closing a cup holder in the back of the car and rolling the window up and down, commenting on all there was to do in this new car. As they passed Evorez's private home, Vanessa noticed several military vehicles lining the road and armed guards standing at the corner. This morning when she left, the road had been empty.

At home, Oliver retreated to his room to play and Vanessa tried to get some news, to figure out what exactly was going on and determine how much she needed to worry. She tried Victor's cell phone and was unsurprised when it went straight to voice mail. He never turned on his phone, and certainly not when he was out on an operation. She checked her computer, but the internet was down. She turned on the television, noticing that all the cable channels were blocked. The only station broadcasting was a government-owned news channel. While Vanessa had read her share of history and knew controlling information was key to taking or holding power, this was the first time she had experienced it firsthand. She found it incredibly unnerving.

"El Toro has taken refuge inside a hospital, where excellent doctors are treating him for wounds suffered when a police demonstration turned violent," said the woman with long, dark hair, too much lipstick, and a look of concern on her face. The screen showed images of the demonstration, police yelling for better wages, and soldiers in full military gear trying to break them up. A few clouds of tear gas hovered around the crowd. "Our leader has determined the police attempted to oust him from power, but with the loyal military's great support, our dear president has put a stop to the conniving interlopers! El Toro is about to speak to his people! We go now to the hospital."

They cut to a shot of the exterior of the hospital. The camera panned along the hospital wall. Vanessa saw a figure leaning out of a window. The camera went close up on the figure, taking a moment to focus, in and out, and then there he was, El Toro, Rafa Evorez, president of Guayandes, halfway out the window, arms raised above him as if he were Eva Perón, gesturing to his people to love him! Love him!

"I have survived!" he yelled. The sound came through perfectly and Vanessa realized he was wearing a microphone. *That's rather convenient for a spur of the moment press conference*, she thought. *Almost as if this were planned.* "To my enemies, I say, here I am! You want me? Here I am! Kill me if you dare!" He pulled at his tie and ripped open his shirt, exposing his chest. A patch of unruly dark hair peeped out. A crowd of supporters had gathered in front of the hospital and cheered El Toro's strength. Vanessa noticed a group of people holding pro-Evorez signs getting off a military bus a moment before the camera turned away. *He's busing supporters in to his own coup*, she thought to herself. *This whole thing is orchestrated.*

He continued yelling from the window, the news channel's anchors dutifully covering every word and expressing fear for their dear leader's safety. A news scroll at the bottom of the screen announced that the government had dispatched military units throughout the city to secure radio towers and military and other government offices.

Evorez, sweating now, finished his speech from the window. "Beginning immediately, I declare a state of emergency throughout the country. A curfew of eight o'clock in the evening is now in effect. I announce that I am giving the military the right to shoot anyone who is out after that time."

Vanessa looked at her watch. It was 6:00 PM. Where was Victor?

***

Victor accelerated backward then spun the car around.

Mike held on to the door. "Maybe the military are there for our protection," he said.

"You didn't get out much in Iraq, did you?" Victor asked. He had seen enough roadblocks to know not to wait.

He swerved around the few oncoming cars, aware for the first time that he was on the wrong side of the highway, but assessing the median—a giant block of concrete—too high for his car to clear.

"We should rethink this, Victor," Mike said. He had one hand on the dashboard and the other on the handle above his door. He looked pale, swaying back and forth as Victor swerved onto the shoulder then back into a lane. Back at the landslide, the car climbed the dirt. Victor went slowly in order not to spin the wheels and descended onto the correct side of the road, gunning it once the tires hit the pavement.

Victor knew there was a detour. Patrón had told him about an unpaved road off the highway that circled around and entered Guayita from the south. "You know where that guy is always selling fishing worms even though there's no river?" Patrón had said. "Past him, right after the cinderblock building that actually has a roof—*not* the one with the satellite dish and no roof—there's a little turn off. You'll be surprised you never noticed it before."

Victor found the turnoff, and they bumped over the unpaved path, descending below the highway. It was narrower than the main road, but since it wound through the valley, they no longer faced death from falling off a sheer cliff. Victor glanced up occasionally, however, to make sure no car had flown off the highway above to come pummeling down on them. They passed a mule, which brayed at them with anger but trotted off the path. Walking along the side of the road was an old couple, neither more than five-feet-tall, wrinkles creasing their browned skin like worn leather. The woman was carrying a large bundle of wood on her back, various sizes of sticks and branches gathered in a blanket that was tied around her waist and shoulders. She stooped under the weight, making her even shorter.

After several minutes, Victor could see they were approaching the city. Groupings of shacks along the road became denser; children ran along the roads laughing, chasing after donkeys and their own little siblings. The car entered a tunnel, which emptied directly into the city. Mike seemed to breathe for the first time since they had left the jungle.

Victor, on the other hand, took one look around and tensed up. An army tank. An armored personnel carrier. A helicopter hovering overhead. Men in uniforms. Too many men in uniforms, Victor thought, one of whom looked like he was about to block Victor's car.

Tired and ready for a shower, Victor remembered a lesson he had learned from Patrón years before and that had served him well in many situations: if you believe you belong somewhere, everyone else will believe it, too. Victor hit the accelerator, drove past the soldier and his cohorts, and floored it past the tank and APC. In his rearview mirror, he could see the soldiers. They watched his car as it disappeared and looked at each other, no one wanting to take responsibility. They did nothing.

The streets were empty after that. In five minutes, they were in front of Mike's house.

"That's not very prudent, what you just did." Mike said.

"Are you home safely?"

"I'm the one who has to deal with the complaint, when the Guayandan military tells the ambassador that one of our cars did not heed a military roadblock, as required under our bilateral diplomatic treaty."

"The soldiers didn't move. Do you really think they care who we are? Something bigger than us is going on. Why don't we focus on that?"

"How can I focus on what's going on here when I have to explain to Director that our field officers can't follow the rules?"

Victor really wanted Mike to get out of the car.

"You'll have to write that cable, Victor," Mike said. He finally opened his door and started to get out. Victor drove off before the door was fully slammed shut. He circled around to his own compound and pulled into his garage.

He stepped out of the car and stretched. He caught a whiff of old garbage then realized he was, in fact, smelling himself. He hauled his duffel bag over his neck and shoulder and headed in to the apartment.

"You missed it!" Vanessa said the moment he walked through the front door. "A coup d'état and you missed it!" She made a repulsed face. "You need a shower."

"Is that what's going on?"

"Wait a minute." Vanessa stood up from the couch where she had been watching the news and faced Victor. "There was a coup d'état and you didn't know it? Who do you work for?"

Victor dropped his bag in the hallway. "We can't know everything instantly."

"Excuses!" she called after him as he walked to the bedroom. "Did you even notice I unpacked the house?"

"Looks great!" he said, without a single glance around.

He took a few minutes to clean up and wrestle with Oliver before he met Vanessa on their terrace with two glasses of wine.

"I'm glad to see you weren't kidnapped," she said. "My lover will be less pleased, but he can wait."

"Always so cheeky," Victor said, clanging his glass against hers. "The house does look nice, by the way. Great color scheme."

"You like the pastels? Does it make you feel like playing golf?"

"I do feel like maybe we've retired to Florida."

"Different shithole, but same idea," Vanessa said.

"At least it's new furniture," he said. "They could have given us used furniture. I saw it in someone else's house. Don't hold a UV light up to it. God knows what DNA samplings you'll find."

Vanessa crinkled her face.

They both took a swig of wine, staring out at the falling night, stars just starting to peek out behind the three volcanoes they could see from their table. A barrage of gunfire broke out, and they both set their glasses down, listening. Given the geography around Guayita, the sound reverberated off the mountains. They didn't know how many shots were real and how many were echoes.

"It's coming from behind us," Victor said after a minute. "Downtown. It's far. We're fine." He picked up his glass.

"A good way to spend a coup," Vanessa said, toasting Victor again.

"Better than my last coup," he said, recalling hiding in a bathtub as a tank shot up his hotel when he experienced a coup in West Africa several years earlier.

"Shouldn't you be doing something?"

"Like what?"

"I don't know. You're a CYA officer in the middle of a coup. It seems like you should be doing more than sitting on your terrace drinking wine."

More gunshots rang out.

"That's probably my source getting shot at right now. Or shooting at someone else. My guess is he doesn't have time to talk. Anyway, I spoke with Patrón. He and Wes have it covered for the short-term. He told me to stay in until tomorrow."

They watched the clouds form over the valley below, the peak of Paxico volcano still visible above. The gunshots tapered off until Guayita was silent, except for the occasional howl of a stray dog.

CHAPTER SIX

Victor pulled up to the embassy the following morning. Thanks to the state of emergency, traffic had been light, but people were still out and about. Other than a tank on one of the main avenues and the noticeable presence of men in uniforms, city life seemed to continue normally.

The embassy, a modern-looking box surrounded by a perimeter wall within a second perimeter wall, had relocated to the outskirts of town the year before and took the architectural concept of form follows function to the extreme. The place was wholly functional, with zero thought for aesthetics. Security was the main driver behind this design: cameras perched everywhere, high walls, and layers of guards and weapons. The face of the US government abroad transformed from welcoming to menacing in the wake of the attacks both on the homeland and on embassies located elsewhere. Despite this, and despite President Evorez's remonstrance against the evil swine up north, the line for visas to go to the United States was as long as ever.

He drove around the parking lot twice looking for a space to park. The planners hadn't realized that moving the embassy out of downtown meant more people would drive rather than take public transportation. Plus the security office had begun warning people against taking public transportation even if it was available, due to the increased number of muggings. Finally, a car started to pull out and Victor raced around to grab the spot. He saw Savannah, the woman who organized events for the embassy community, in the driver's seat. She wore giant sunglasses and a pink cowboy hat. She waved and rolled down her window, unwilling to give Victor the spot until he put in some good face time with her.

"I met your lovely wife!" she chirped. "I do hope she'll join the crafts committee! You really should encourage her to get more involved." She gave Victor a sad weepy face.

Victor assured her he would, even though he knew Vanessa would reject any community bonding. He would say anything to get Savannah out of that parking spot so he could get to his office.

He entered through the different security checkpoints, flashing his embassy badge and chatting amicably with the guards.

"How's Messi?" one guard asked him. The guy had seen Oliver, once, in a Lionel Messi soccer jersey and had asked about the boy every day since.

Victor gave his standard response, "That's my retirement plan."

"Ha! Retirement plan!" the guard laughed on cue.

Victor went to the door of Guayita Station and placed his phone in a wooden box outside the office. Cell phones were not allowed inside, for fear of listening in, tracking movements, or any other dastardly trick the United States would apply to others but never wanted used against itself.

Victor punched in the door's cipher code and entered what Vanessa had come to call the Men's Locker Room. The office was like any other CYA station, except that here, all the officers were male, lending a decidedly testosterone-infused atmosphere to what was already an alpha male environment, filled as it was with guns and plans to kill bad guys.

Like any office, it was a maze of beige partitioned cubicles, but here, desks were accented with booty from the war against the FRPT: a tribal whacking stick, carved with symbolic totems to keep away bad *joojoo*; an FRPT lapel pin, taken by a source from the corpse of an FRPT general killed in a Tamindoan military airstrike guided by the CYA; a large chart with the photos of all the FRPT leaders. Those who had been terminated had a large red X crossing out their picture. At the top of the chart sat Paulo Reis, whose black-and-white photo showed him in a military cap with a cigar in his mouth. There was no red X.

The Latin beats of a Reggaeton dance mix greeted Victor, quiet but still pulsing from the office speakers, a sound-masking technique in case anyone tried to place a listening device nearby. "Turn this shit off," he said to no one in particular, since he couldn't see anyone. All at once, his colleagues popped out of the cubicle farm like prairie dogs from the dirt.

"Hey!"

"*¡Hola!*"

"Don't fuck with Reggaeton."

"How'd it go?" asked Simon. He pronounced his name the Spanish way, *See-mone*, even though he grew up in Des Moines. Simon Sands was the station's tech guru. He could barely operate his iPhone, but if an officer needed a beacon that was also a listening device with a four-day battery that could withstand being dragged through pouring rain and mud, Simon was the man to see.

"Mike couldn't find the meeting site," Victor said, "but Frank covered me. I got good info, but El Gordo needs some more reassurance."

"He couldn't find the meeting site? Kiltoa is a fucking grid," said Wes. He rubbed his hand over his shaved head. A former Marine, Wes Carter's body was compact and tight and held enough potential energy to break a table in half. He was a pit bull, man's best friend unless someone fucked with him.

"I can slow down his travel reimbursement, if it makes you feel any better," said Andy Rollins. Although he ingested more caffeine than seemed safe for a human and his hair was in a constant state of what Victor could only describe as "electrified cool," Andy was that rare CYA creature: a support officer who knew how to support officers.

"What's the deal with this coup?" Victor asked.

"It wasn't a coup." All eyes turned as Patrón emerged from his office.

The chief of station had earned his moniker because he looked like the dashing spokesman from the Patrón tequila commercials. In each commercial, the bearded spokesman relayed an insane adventure. Patrón was an old school spy who had actually *lived* insane adventures. He had lived and worked in several denied areas—countries whose internal security services made life difficult for any spy trying to operate there—and could maintain a sense of playfulness even when local authorities would confront him with seemingly incontrovertible proof of his deeds.

Once, when a KGB officer caught him skinny-dipping with Boris Yeltsin's daughter in Norway, he had castigated the man for allowing the young lady out of his sight. "She should never have been allowed out here to go swimming in the first place. What will your superiors say when they find out you lost sight of her?" He was the personification of the Agency's unofficial motto, "Admit nothing. Deny everything. Make counter-accusations."

Patrón also really liked tequila. "Only white tequila," he reminded people. "Dark tequila swells my uvula. That was a bad thing to discover in a lean-to in Nepal with only a mule nearby."

Victor knew he could work for Patrón and could trust him. The two had worked together years ago on a Beirut operation, which had involved various disguises, including one with fishnet stockings. Talk about trust. While cleaning up after the operation, Patrón had said off-handedly to Victor, "Did I ever tell you how I ended up delivering Muammar Qaddafi's index finger in a box to Director?"

This established trust combined with Patrón's penchant for adventure had been one of the main reasons Victor had agreed to go to Guayandes to begin with. Besides being ready for a break from the war on terror, he had agreed to give South America a chance because Patrón had asked him to.

On one of Victor's first nights in Guayita, Patrón had taken him to a bar to discuss what he wanted from Victor for the coming two years. In the middle of waxing poetic about the FRPT's waning commitment to Marxist ideologies—"They're buying tents from REI. I mean, talk about bourgeois," he was saying—a flash of sexy turned Patrón's eye, as if a large diamond had caught the light and blinded him.

At the end of the bar was a stunning, dark-skinned beauty with long, blown out, platinum blonde hair. Her dark eyebrows confessed that blonde was not her natural color. Victor guessed that was not her natural cleavage either. But Patrón didn't mind.

"That's Miss Guayandes," Patrón said, explaining that she was the most recent winner of the country's most prestigious beauty pageant. The entire country took the pageant very seriously. The finals were broadcast on state television on a Saturday night, every bar and restaurant and home tuned in to the glitzy display of well-oiled, tanned skin around tight, bulging, calf, breast, and butt implants, as if nipping and tucking were national pastimes to be treasured forever. Victor half expected to see the names of plastic surgeons on each contestant's sash, like corporate branding. "Dr. Mendez presents, Miss Guayita!"

Victor had subsequently learned that Frank, before taking up permanent residence in the jungle, had once been a judge for the Miss Guayandes contest, the year a woman named Maria had won. Well, one of the years a woman named Maria had won. Victor now knew the winner almost every year was named Maria-something, Maria-Elena, Maria-Fernanda, Maria-Cristina. The list was long. Victor had never managed to learn exactly *how* Frank had become a judge for the pageant. The fact of it was now Agency lore, but no one seemed to know the details.

Patrón smiled at the shiny blonde at the bar. She smiled back and asked, chin down, big eyes looking up through long, mascaraed lashes, "Do I know you?"

In perfect Spanish, Patrón responded, "Last weekend. Under the waterfall and the full moon."

The woman claimed not to remember.

"I'm pretty sure it was you," Patrón said, enjoying being teased. "Although you've dyed your hair since then."

Her face lit up, as she understood the mix up. "My sister," she explained. "I have an identical twin sister."

At that moment, as Victor had started to say to himself, *No fucking way*, the woman's twin sister, Miss Guayandes herself, walked into the bar, identical except for her natural dark hair. She recognized Patrón immediately and greeted him with kisses on both of his white, furry cheeks. Victor watched in awe. Patrón was a natural operator, in every sense of the word, and Victor felt almost a fatherly pride when he left the bar, Patrón squeezing into a booth between Miss Guayandes and her identical twin sister.

That's not to say Patrón hadn't had his challenges at the CYA. Indeed, he had come to Guayandes as a sort of break, a way to fly under the radar until the politics at Director changed, as they inevitably would, as they already had, which was why Patrón had found himself in the middle of a shitstorm that required retreat to a rather remote corner of Latin America in the first place. He was a controversial figure at Director. Then again, anyone who had been doing this for as long as Patrón had was bound to have done something controversial at some point in his career. It was inevitable in an organization whose officers took risks and when society chose to measure yesterday's actions by today's standards. When the political winds at Director did change, Patrón found himself thoroughly squashed by the proverbial bus Director had chosen to throw him under in order to wrap up the whole episode neatly and move on. Patrón accepted he would take the fall, but rather than stick around Director until retirement and try to make amends, he embraced his pariah status and moved to a shithole where he could run his own show. Victor respected Patrón.

Standing before his team in the Men's Locker Room, Patrón poured a few drops from a leather flask into his coffee mug before explaining what he had learned about the coup the day before. He took a swig directly from the flask before setting it down. He stirred his coffee.

"I got a message from VZHUNTER last night," he said, referring to one of his sources. "The police never planned to oust Evorez. Their demonstration was just that: a demonstration. Evorez provoked the violence in order to declare a state of emergency."

"Two soldiers were shot. One was killed," Victor said.

"Collateral damage, but it serves Evorez's purpose. He'll make them heroes in the revolutionary struggle."

"Does the ambassador know?"

"Not yet. I want corroboration before I go to the ambo."

"VZSURFER?" Victor asked.

"Trigger an emergency meeting. See what he says. Take Adam with you. Show him around town. Where's Mike?"

"He called to say he's afraid to come out during the state of emergency," said Simon.

Patrón started to say something, decided not to, and picked up his flask and returned to his office.

Victor, his backpack still hanging on his shoulder, sunglasses and car key in hand since he hadn't made it to his desk yet, said, "Who the fuck is Adam?"

A young man whom Victor had not noticed poking up from one of the cubicles said, "Um, I'm Adam." He smiled nervously and looked at everyone looking at him. He had been standing there the whole time. "Hi." He waved. He had a thick beard, but Victor could see a baby face under it. The kid looked fresh out of the Farm, the Agency's training facility.

"He got here yesterday," Simon said. He pronounced the *y* like a *j*, so it sounded like he said "jesterday." He had no accent when he said the other words.

Victor sized up Adam and said, "Get your shit. Let's go trigger a meeting."

Adam Greene jumped to his desk and disappeared in his cube for a moment then reappeared in front of Victor. He had on good walking shoes and carried a bottle of water. The kid was ready.

They headed toward the office door, which swung open as they reached it.

"Hey, Victor. I got something for you guys."

"What have you been listening to this time, Sergio?"

Sergio Vidal worked behind an unmarked door on the fifth floor of a building that officially had only four floors. If anyone asked what he did, he would say simply, "Communications." He was fluent in several languages, including Spanish, and had a knack for all things related to computers. While Victor would struggle to print a Word document, Sergio could hack a satellite's computer to reprogram the direction it was facing to help him get better Cinemax at home. He and Victor had done a short stint together in Mali a few years back. Victor recalled Sergio explaining he had volunteered but couldn't understand when he received his travel orders. "I thought they said Bali, dude! I wanted to go to Bali! I had to look up Mali on a map!" He had then spent the majority of the project telling Victor about his plan to become a Walmart greeter in his retirement. "No more computer screens, man. Face-to-face contact with real people, and low prices, too."

Victor had been pleasantly surprised to find out he'd be working with Sergio again in Guayandes. Over the past year spent between Guayandes and Director, they had managed to put together a program that allowed them to listen to nearly all FRPT communications. Sergio and his officers had covertly infiltrated the computers of Kapokom, the only mobile phone company that provided service in the jungle. Through the ECHO program, as it was known internally, they had been collecting intelligence on who was talking to whom about what and for how long for months now and it was proving extremely useful information as Victor and his colleagues looked at options to deal with the narco group.

"We got a readout on El Toro's phone calls from the hospital. Do you want to know one of the first phones his phone was in contact with while this police demonstration was going on?" He waved a single piece of paper over his head. "Paulo Reis."

"The leader of the FRPT is in direct contact with the president of Guayandes?" asked Adam.

"Oh, shit," said Victor.

"Thanks, Sergio," said Patrón as he took the paper. "Victor, Adam, go trigger the meeting. The rest of you, in my office."

***

Victor and Adam jumped into Victor's car and pulled out of the embassy parking lot. Adam looked ready to explode with excitement.

"My first emergency trigger," he said to Victor. "My first anything, actually."

"First tour?" Victor asked.

"I finished training two months ago. I was supposed to come straight down here but there were some problems getting my visa."

"Fucking Evorez," Victor said, "making us jump through hoops to get a fucking visa. What happened?"

"No, not Evorez. The admin officer handling my case at Director worked on a super maxi-flex schedule."

"What the fuck is that?"

"He only worked on Tuesdays. Twenty-four hours straight on Tuesdays, with every eighty-seventh Tuesday off."

They drove on in silence for a few minutes, Adam fidgeting in his seat, his eyes darting from window to window, absorbing all the sights of the city like an excited child.

"What are we going to do exactly?" Adam asked, unable to contain himself. "A four-hour surveillance detection route split between walking on foot and driving in the car? Mark a tree with a piece of chalk? Or we can signal him with a piece of fruit in the windshield. That's what we did in training. I always carry a banana with me." He pulled a bruised banana out of his backpack. "Or do you have a drop site? That's it, isn't it? We're heading toward the park to drop a note in the hollow of a tree. I knew it! It's so exciting! I'm glad I wore my good shoes! I don't look too obvious, do I?"

"We're going to call him."

"What?" The excitement drained out of Adam's face, replaced with disappointment. Victor had parked and Adam looked around. They were in the parking lot of Radio Shack.

"Go in and buy a disposable phone. Pay cash. I'll wait here."

"That's the commo plan? Buy a phone and call him?"

"That's it. Sorry it's not sexier. It's just easier." He watched Adam droop out of the car and drag himself into Radio Shack. He returned a few minutes later with a prepaid, disposable cell phone. They pulled out of the parking lot and headed toward Adam's apartment. At a stoplight, Victor sent a text message then ripped the battery out of the phone.

Victor pulled over in an alley a few blocks from Adam's place. "Be ready at eight AM sharp tomorrow. We're hiking, so plan accordingly." He got out of the car and placed the phone under one of the wheels. He got back in and backed up, running over the phone and smashing it. He went forward to run it over one more time. He got out again, picked up the pieces, handed a few to Adam and said, "Toss those into different trash cans on your way home. I'll take care of these parts." He drove off, leaving Adam standing on the side of a dusty road contemplating the demolished device in his hand.

CHAPTER SEVEN

Victor arrived home to his Florida retirement pad and found Vanessa gathering her purse and keys, preparing to go out with Oliver.

"Back to school night," she said.

"He's only been in school three days with all the closings. How can he be going *back*? It's more like *finally* going to school night. And what about the state of emergency?"

"Curfew is at eight, which means we're lucky because the school won't be able to drag the event out for hours and hours. You coming or not?"

Victor shrugged and followed her and Oliver out the door.

Meeting the parents of Oliver's friends had been a strange endeavor from the start. Back in Washington, the international environment of his school combined with his parents' hyper aware-ness of and sensitivity to counterintelligence threats had made it hard for either of them to—as a teacher would put it—play nicely with the other parents. It didn't help that, after Oliver's birth, Ness had returned to the Bureau to a counterintelligence position tracking Russian illegals. One suspected couple lived in Victor and Vanessa's building. Victor was no better. On walks through town, the two of them would remark on faces they saw more than once. On drives out to the ocean, they would memorize license plates. They didn't *mean* to do it. They just did it.

So meeting new people was always a challenge. They loved the act of meeting new people, that wasn't the problem. But each new person needed to be thoroughly vetted before either of them would open up. Until then, they would keep conversations superficial.

They tried to make it fun, too. They would give each other challenges before going to a social event. Five points for figuring out the host's middle name. Ten for nailing down his or her most intimate ailments. It kept their elicitation skills sharp. Other times, they gave each other random hobbies, without warning. In the middle of a conversation, Ness would say to the host, "Victor has been volunteering at the elephant house at the zoo." Without skipping a beat, Victor would launch into a lecture about the magnificence of elephants. They simply couldn't help it.

They arrived at the school and went through security and headed to the auditorium. Ellie and Simon were standing in the lobby, Ellie chatting with other parents and Simon looking bored. Ellie and Vanessa hugged. Simon and Victor shook hands, nodded, and said, "Hey."

"Get a nametag!" Ellie said with her usual enthusiasm. "Simon, where's yours?"

"Ellie, I keep telling you. Down here, it's pronounced *See-mone*."

"You're from Des Moines! And your last name is Sands."

"That's the Anglicization of Sanz."

"You'll know you've made it in Guayandes when she calls you Jorge," said Vanessa.

Victor leaned over the nametag table and scribbled with a Sharpie before sticking the label on Oliver's T-shirt.

"Eugene DuPont?" Vanessa said, looking at the nametag. "What the fuck, Victor?" Oliver looked at his nametag for a microsecond, spied his friends, and took off toward them, unaware, or unconcerned, that he was now Eugene DuPont.

"It's good training," Victor said and gave his wife a charming smile that made her want to kiss him and smack him at the same time.

They followed Ellie and Simon into the auditorium and sat down.

As the principal of the school stepped on stage, Victor scanned the audience. He saw several families from the embassy, but also many wealthy local Guayandan families. If they could afford to send their children here, they were part of the country's elite, and were thus likely to be well connected politically. He took mental notes of their faces. They were all potential targets.

Vanessa could see Victor calculating. "This is your son's school," she said to him as a warning. "Do you understand what that means? It means—"

"It means easy access." He smiled and went back to assessing the pool of targets. Vanessa rolled her eyes. She looked at Oliver, sitting a few seats down with his friends. He had placed his nametag sticker on his forehead.

The principal flipped through Power Point slides and droned on about the school's finances before launching into a monologue about how the school was creating Global Leaders. The Power Point slide showed those words, Global Leaders, with a capital *G* and capital *L*. Even without the visual aid, Vanessa could hear the capital letters in the way the principal said the phrase.

"We are creating Global Leaders, responsible citizens of the world who will shape our future." Vanessa and Victor looked at their son, with a Eugene DuPont nametag stuck to his forehead, knocking his head on the seat in front of him while he said, "Butt! Butt! Butt!" over and over and his friends laughed. Victor and Vanessa gave each other a warm smile. Their son was indeed Global Leader material.

In the lobby afterward, Vanessa did her best to mingle with the other parents, which meant standing next to Ellie and allowing her to introduce her to people. Victor and Simon stood on the side, observing.

"Hello, *chicas*!"

Ellie and Vanessa both turned to see Savannah running toward them with open arms. She was wearing a jacket that was covered in pink fur—or were those feathers?—and she enveloped the women in a fuzzy pink hug. Vanessa choked on a feather as she pulled away.

"We're going to have lots of school activities this year! We need lots of parent involvement to make our kids' experience extra special. I know I can count on you. Right?" She looked at Ellie who smiled. "Right?" She looked at Vanessa, who was still pulling pink fluff out of her mouth. "Who wants to sign up to bake a hundred and sixty cupcakes for next week's Teacher Appreciation Day?"

Oliver came tearing through the crowd with a little girl with dark braids. His Eugene DuPont sticker was back on his shirt, upside down. "Slow down!" yelled Vanessa, using the distraction to move away from Savannah.

An elegant woman in designer jeans, a chic peasant top, and very high heel suede shoes asked, "Is that your son? He and my daughter are in the same class. Eugene is it?"

Vanessa gave Victor a quick sideways glance. He smiled. "Oliver," Vanessa said.

"Cristiana is also in Miss Natalia's class. I've seen your son there a few times."

Vanessa felt a small pang of guilt. After the Lunch Bunch fiasco, she hadn't been able to bring herself to go to any parent events at the school. She had come to back to school night only because she wanted to see Oliver's classroom projects. If she were a good mother, she told herself, she'd already know this woman. She heard Savannah trying to get Ellie to sign up to make vegan icing for the one hundred sixty cupcakes. "You can buy the ingredients at the commissary."

Vanessa figured this woman couldn't be any worse. She stuck out her hand. "Vanessa."

"Claudette," said the woman.

"Do I detect an accent? Or more specifically, a not Guayandan accent."

"Belgian," Claudette responded. "I moved here several years ago for my husband's work."

Another dependent, Vanessa thought, and followed with the standard questions. "How long is your posting here? Where do you go next?"

"We live here permanently. My husband is from Guayandes. We met at university in the States, but we live here now." Cristiana, her braids swinging, grabbed her mother's leg. "We must go now, but it was a pleasure to meet you, Vanessa. I'm sure we'll see each other around." Claudette leaned in conspiratorially. "Although, I won't be providing a hundred sixty cupcakes." She winked and grabbed Cristiana's hand. "Have a good evening."

Vanessa laughed and watched them leave.

CHAPTER EIGHT

The sky was a perfect blue and opened up in front of Victor and Adam as they drove out of Guayita and descended into the valley. The state of emergency was still in effect, but the few soldiers on the road were content to let cars pass while they ate yucca bread and napped.

Two hours outside of town, Victor pulled off the highway onto a tiny dirt path that was barely visible from the main road. The first few meetings Victor had had with VZSURFER, he had missed the turnoff until he learned the exact shape of the boulder that sat right before it. They tumbled along and rounded a hill, after which the great Paxico volcano rose above them. Normally shrouded in clouds, today the volcano stood majestically under the clear sky, its glaciered peak twinkling in the sun. It looked exactly like a volcano Oliver, or any six-year-old, would draw: a perfectly symmetrical mountain with the top shaved off, white snow cascading down the top before giving way to the brown-and-gray silt.

Around the volcano, the ground was desolate, dark earth scourged by the lava of thousands of eruptions, volcanic rocks littering the vast space. Victor could see three men on horse-back in the distance, riding in the direction of a nearby haci-enda. He stopped near the base of the volcano and turned off the car.

"Ready for a hike?" He got out of the car and adjusted his brown leather vest.

Adam slid out of the passenger seat and fiddled with his back-pack. "Should I put this banana in the windshield?" He saw Victor's face and put the banana back in his bag. "Ready."

He followed Victor up a path that was hidden behind some crunchy bushes and rocks. The volcanic soot gave way under their feet. Each footstep went deep into the ground and raised a puff of dust, like walking on sand. A hawk circled overhead. They marched in near silence for half an hour, at which point their bodies warmed up and their labored breathing finally relaxed.

They came to the top of a hill. Victor peered over the side. Adam followed suit. There, they saw a man hiking up from the other side. Victor turned to Adam, punched his thumb in the direction of the approaching man, and said, "VZSURFER. I call him Fernandez." Victor thought Adam's head would explode with excitement and he kind of envied how green the kid was.

"*Amigo*," Fernandez said, shaking Victor's hand. He was dressed in drab cargo pants and a sweatshirt, a rugged canvas backpack on his shoulders. He had leathery skin and looked like the military man he was, tall and solid, thick in the shoulders, and fit.

"I'm glad to see you weren't shot," Victor said, offering Fernandez a cigarette. They were at more than 14,000 feet in altitude and Adam wondered how they were going to manage to smoke.

Fernandez lit up and took a long, hearty drag before releasing a cloud of smoke. "It got out of control. Evorez wanted a show but he didn't plan the shooting."

"How did it go down?"

"The police had planned the demonstration. We knew about that, days before. The day of the demonstration, Evorez decided to confront them. He knew he was poking a bear. But he also knew the police had no designs on his power. They want their salaries. They weren't organized to overthrow him. That was never part of the plan. But Evorez knew it would make good TV. Rattle the hornets' nest, take a hit, smash the hornets, look like the hero." He took another drag. "Then declare a state of emergency. Consolidate your power. I had gone to the protest site with him, but he didn't call for the military backup until people started shooting. I don't think he planned on calling it an attempted coup. He wanted to look like a strong leader. But when the opportunity arose to blame the other side, he took it. Segundo made sure of that."

Victor knew Segundo Espina was President Evorez's closest adviser. He asked, "Who shot first? And why?"

"Evorez. He shot in the air to clear the protest." Fernandez took another puff on his cigarette. "It wasn't the most thought out plan, but it did the trick."

"Did he get shot?"

"No. He was taken away pretty fast, to the hospital, which conveniently had microphones and television cameras ready to capture his rescue. No one was allowed in his room except certain journalists. Even the doctors weren't allowed on his floor."

"It was orchestrated."

"He saw the opportunity and he took it. Now, he can pull the reins of power." He made a squeezing gesture with his fist.

Victor reached into his backpack and pulled out an envelope, which he handed to Fernandez, who slid it into a pocket. Fernandez took a last drag on the cigarette, stubbed it out on the bottom of his boot, and shoved the butt into a different pocket. He shook Victor's hand again, gave a curt nod in Adam's direction, and marched back down the hill. He wound a curve and disappeared out of sight. Adam finally exploded.

"That was awesome!" He stood with his hand up in the air, waiting for Victor to give him a high five. Victor blinked at him and started down the path they had come up. Adam chased after him. "You can't leave me hanging here. You can't. Come on. One high five."

He reminded Victor of Oliver, a child who finally gets someone to give in through sheer repetition and annoyance but whose glee in doing so is endearing enough to force a smile and, in this case, a high five. Victor really admired the kid's enthusiasm. His own had succumbed to cynicism years ago. Adam was a nice reminder of how fun this life could be.

Adam chatted incessantly during the hike back to the car. He replayed every detail of what, to Victor, had been a routine meeting. "We all arrived at the meeting location at *exactly* the same time," he said. "I can't believe he even *found* the meeting location. It's a huge volcano. How did you know where to find each other? What did you say to him? 'Meet me on the path by the bushes'?" He kept going, trying to figure out how Victor and Fernandez each knew the exact location in the middle of a giant national park.

They arrived at the car and Victor threw the keys to Adam. He had only come back from the jungle two days ago and, despite the Fernandez meeting's being routine, any source meeting required a certain level of organization and stress. He was tired. "You drive," he said to Adam.

Adam made two fists and pulled his elbows in toward his sides, a movement of triumph as he said, "Yes!" under his breath. He clambered up into the driver's seat and double-checked the four-wheel drive.

Victor slid down in the passenger seat and closed his eyes. He could feel the rough ground under the car as they bumped along, the bouncing lulling him closer and closer to sleep. He fell into the abyss.

"Oh, shit!"

Victor shuddered awake. His hand instinctively went to his hip, where his gun was. Adam slammed on the brakes, as Victor assessed the situation. Directly in front of them was a group of people swarming the car. Their faces were covered with brightly colored masks. As Victor gathered his wits, he realized they weren't ski masks, but papier-mâché, tied around the heads of the descending crowd. Some had elongated noses or exaggerated chins, sharp cheekbones or bulbous foreheads. Some of the menacing mob had stretched a thick rope in front of the car, forming a roadblock, and many held what looked like AK-47s.

"They want to kidnap us!" Adam yelled.

Victor was about to speak when Adam, high on adrenaline, threw the car into reverse and floored it. In textbook combat driving style, he didn't turn around but used the rearview mirror to see where he was going, then swung the car a hundred eighty degrees around, all in a single, smooth movement, before tearing forward again.

Adam was breathing quickly. "We're off the X. Holy shit! We're off the X!"

Victor glanced at the side mirror. They were indeed out of the area of danger, but as they peeled away, some of the would-be kidnappers took off their masks, confirming Victor's suspicions. "They're children," he said.

"What?" Adam said, turning to Victor. He was still breathing fast.

"They're kids. It's a tradition around here at this time of year. They wear masks, hold up cars, and ask for money. It's supposed to be in good fun."

"What kind of a fucking tradition is that?" Adam yelled, hitting the steering wheel with the palm of his hand. "Guayandes is the fucking kidnap capital of the world! And they make a tradition out of *fake* kidnappings? What about their guns?"

"Sticks, painted to look like guns." Victor chuckled as the tension dispersed. "Good driving, though. I'm guessing you passed the combat driving course no problem."

Adam brooded as he drove. After a minute he said, "It's a stupid fucking tradition."

Victor laughed again. "Don't sweat it. You did the right thing."

"I feel like an asshole."

"Don't. You're right, it's a stupid fucking tradition."

"You've never made a mistake like that."

"I've made plenty of mistakes like that."

"You're the great Victor Caro. You're a legend at Director. Everyone talks about you."

"Everyone talks about wanting to fire me, maybe."

"That, too. But most of it was positive. One of my trainers told me you once held off a rabid dog with a bobble-head Jesus in the middle of a war."

"Habibi was one of your trainers? That must have been tough. I bet he fucked with you nonstop."

"You know Habibi?"

"He's my closest friend," Victor said, recalling the many adventures he and Habibi had had together since first meeting in training, so many years ago. "We've been through a lot together. We had to steal an office car to make that asset meeting where the dog attacked us. How was he as an instructor?"

"Once, I was on my way to an asset meeting I had triggered by placing a banana in the windshield. The asset never showed. When I got back to the car, the banana was gone. When I got back to the training center . . ."

"Habibi was eating your banana?"

Adam nodded.

"Don't worry, he only adds challenges like that for people he knows are good." He glanced at Adam. Adam looked forlorn.

"Look, kid. That's part of the game. We all fuck up sometimes. My first tour, I was in Burundi. We had a source that one of our Non-Official Cover officers had been handling. The NOC had to leave the country. The chief asked me to take over and reactivate the source. So I call him, explain I'm from the US Embassy and can he meet? 'Sure,' he says, and we arrange for me to go to his office the next day. I show up, thinking we'll have a private conversation. I'll explain the NOC is gone and can he keep up the work but do it for me? But he didn't understand. He thought I really was coming from the US Embassy, and he called in every fucking journalist and TV camera in Bujumbura to advertise that Uncle Sam wanted a strategic partnership with his organization."

"Holy shit. What did you do?"

"I pledged a million dollars in US aid and smiled for the cameras. When I went into the office the next day, the guys had plastered copies of the newspaper story, complete with a photo of me shaking our source's hand, all over the station."

"Did we have to give a million dollars?"

"No, once I got him alone and explained who I was, he felt really bad for the misunderstanding. He became a really good source. But I'm sure there's a YouTube clip of that press conference somewhere. So you see? We all fuck up."

Adam let this sink in and they drove on in silence for a few minutes.

"You liked how I drove?"

"You got off the X. Textbook."

With one hand on the steering wheel, Adam made his triumphant gesture with the other hand. "Yes!"

CHAPTER NINE

"We need to build on the momentum of the last few days, *Señor Presidente*. The people loved your strong display against the disloyal police. We need to seize the moment to advance the revolution."

Segundo was standing in his usual spot in front of President Evorez's desk. Evorez, dressed in his colorful sweat suit, bit into a salami sandwich and tossed a miniature basketball into a hoop hanging off the back of one of the doors. A buzzer on his desk rang. He took another bite of his sandwich before he clicked the button. Crumbs rained down on the buzzer. His secretary came on the speaker.

"*Señor Presidente*, you have a call from a *Señor* Juarez."

Evorez looked at Segundo with wide, expectant eyes. Juarez was Paulo Reis's code name. Segundo gave a slight nod of his head. "Put him through," Evorez said.

"My dear president, it appears your state of emergency is going well. It is quite a masterful demonstration of your awesome powers."

"You are too kind, general." Evorez paused. "Feel free to continue!"

"I have long studied leadership, sir. You are an inspiration. With Your Excellency at the helm, the revolution is sure to succeed. We feel confident you will prevail in the upcoming election."

Evorez was giddy. Segundo smiled. He liked where this was heading.

"We feel the fervor up north here, too, El Toro. Many of my men are anxious to support the revolution from here."

Segundo interjected before Evorez could respond. "What a kind offer, general. We'll be drawing up a list of our many overlapping priorities."

"Excellent," Reis said. "You'll be pleased to hear, as well, Dear Leader, one of my lieutenants reported to me this morning that he saw a bull painted on a wall in town, under the words *¡Viva El Toro!* Your support is only growing."

"The people love me!" Evorez said to Segundo after they hung up. Segundo was pleased Reis's men were painting pictures of bulls on walls all over the northern regions of Guayandes, as Segundo had instructed. The most important part of being a great leader, he knew, was to be perceived as being a great leader.

"*Señor Presidente*, I have arranged for you to visit a Guayandes Petroleum dig site in the jungle. It will be good for the workers to see your face in the wake of the recent labor changes you implemented."

"Have we managed to hire twenty thousand patriots to replace the subversive workers I fired?"

"We are well on our way. Additionally, several more murals of El Toro have gone up around the city."

"You see? They really do love me! I am sure to win this election!"

"As you know, sir, this is also *corrida* season."

"I love a good bullfight, Segundo." Evorez stood up and pranced around his office. "The matador swings the cape and *yupi*!" He pretended to swing a cape and danced with an imaginary bull that was circling him. "In go the *banderillas*, into the bull's shoulders!" Evorez swooped his arm, as though lancing the bull. He stared into the pretend bull's eyes. He was breathing heavily. "The bull weakens, until the matador," Evorez flung his pretend cape, "lures him closer in order to," Evorez was on his tippy toes with one arm in the air, "slide the sword in to pierce the beast's heart." Evorez swung his arm down as though stabbing the bull. "And down goes the bull. *El toro* is dead." He stared at his imagined dead bull on the ground. His breathing started to slow and a look of concern crossed his face. Evorez looked up at Segundo. "Wait a minute. *I* am El Toro. Why do these matadors want to kill me?" He looked again at his imaginary bull in a heap. "We must stop the *corrida*!"

Segundo put his hands on Evorez's shoulders. The president was nearly hyperventilating. Segundo led him to the couch and sat him down.

"Your Excellency, you know I would never lead you astray. I have a plan for your *corrida*."

CHAPTER TEN

Victor searched his office for a pen, pushing aside dirty coffee mugs, four separate cell phones with their batteries pulled, and a small wooden hippo statue that a source in Zimbabwe had given him years ago. He looked behind a glass bowl of potpourri Andy had given him after a particularly bad exchange with Director. Director had sent Victor a cable asking him to fill out a database with his emergency contact information. Victor had explained to Director that he had already filled out that database, but Director replied that this was a new database, specifically for Latin America. Victor had inquired why Director could not simply export the information from one database to the other, and Director had responded with a lengthy cable with technical explanations. Andy had heard Victor screaming in frustration and found him poised to chuck a Director coffee mug at his computer. Andy had placed the bowl of potpourri on Victor's desk and said, "Stay chill, dude. I got this." Victor now kept the bowl under the FRPT kill list with the red Xs.

He finally found a pen under his desk. He grabbed it and a scrap piece of paper and made his way to the station conference room.

The rest of the Men's Locker Room was already there. Wes, Simon, Mike, and Adam were staring at Patrón, enraptured. Adam's mouth was slightly open.

"And that's how I ended up with Abu Nidal's underwear," Patrón said. He turned as Victor entered. "Great, you're here. We can get started." He began filling plastic cups with Johnnie Walker Black and handing them around the table. The guys each took a cup and took a sip.

"It tastes good at ten in the morning," Mike said. "I can't say I've ever had whiskey so early before." The others looked at him, wondering what was wrong with him.

"Here are a few truths," Patrón said. "One miscalculation, one misperception, and a war could break out. We still don't know what the FRPT is aiming for. A reprieve from Tamindo? Or state sponsorship from Guayandes? The drawbacks for US policy in Latin America would be huge if the FRPT were getting concrete support from the government of Guayandes. As you all know, the cocaine grown and processed here makes its way up to the United States. The money that comes back fuels more violence down here. The instability of Guayandes doesn't help things. The election only adds to that instability."

He took a deep breath before continuing. "The Guayandan economy is tanking. I know. It's hard to believe that firing all the engineers and researchers from the country's top industry and replacing them with your cronies might have adverse effects, but, well, sometimes socialism has its downsides. Evorez's firing of half the workers at Guayandes Petroleum has—you'll all be shocked to hear this—led to a massive decrease in output. With less oil to export, the country can't get its hands on foreign currency, namely the US dollar. The only export the country has left is sardines. That is also problematic, since they have to import the nets to catch the sardines they export." Patrón took a sip of whiskey.

"What about avocados?" asked Mike.

"Fine," Patrón conceded. "They export some avocados, but it's minimal. Guayandes isn't exactly the powerhouse of South America. I'd estimate they export somewhere around eight avocados a year. Most of what they grow is for domestic consumption. Bottom line, if you don't export oil, you don't get hard cash. If you don't have hard cash, you can't buy imports. No oil cash. No nets. No sardines. Even less cash. The economy tanks, and soon, you are left with only avocados to eat." He looked at Mike. "On the border, possibly over the border, is a narco insurgency flush with drug money looking to expand its base. We already know the FRPT is crossing over the border, and Reis looks like he might want to build a relationship with Evorez, who is taking steps to consolidate his power. Several sources have told us that he plans to use the so-called coup to fire the chief of police and place them under his direct command. Does anyone find this problematic?"

They all did. Except Mike.

"Wait a minute," Mike said. "Everything you're talking about sounds real important and all, but is it meeting Director's metrics?"

Everyone around the conference table lifted their cups and drank.

Mike continued, "I hear a lot of 'stopping drugs from reaching the US' and 'maintaining stability.'" He made air quotes while he said those phrases. "But I hear nothing about how many reports we can get out of that."

"What are you getting at?" asked Victor.

"We need an increased number of reports to demonstrate to Director that we've infiltrated the target. More reports means more information." He slowed down his words and looked at his colleagues as he said, "*That's* what's going to get us noticed."

The guys looked at each other then back at Mike, except Patrón, who refilled his cup.

"You're right," said Wes finally. "How could we have been thinking so narrowly, looking to 'maintain stability' and stop a country in the US's backyard from turning into a narco-state?" He made air quotes, too. "Am I right, guys?" He looked around the table. Victor, Simon, Adam, and Patrón stayed quiet and smiled, giving him tacit approval to continue poking fun at Mike. "What do you have in mind to wow Director and get us noticed, before the next promotion panel, I presume?"

"Of course, before the next promotion panel!" Mike said. He was enthusiastic now that he felt he had the guys on his side. He leaned forward, both hands above the table to help emphasize what he was saying. He paused and nearly froze, moving his eyes back and forth, building the anticipation in the room until he finally broke. "Cultivated crop security in the southwest region." He slapped the table and leaned back in his chair and looked like he really wanted to add the word, "Booya!"

"What security where?" asked Adam.

"It's moved up on the priority matrix. I talked with the analyst who handles food security in semiarid coastal flatlands in the southwestern hemisphere. She's been following this for a

decade and says she has some major gaps that need to be filled."
He looked at his notes. "I really think we should concentrate
on this guy who is in charge of cacao beans for the local village
council. Easy recruitment. I've got a few others. I think we can
spread it out to make sure everyone gets their recruitment for
the year."

"What the fuck are you talking about?" said Wes.

"Food security."

"Mike, we're supposed to recruit people because they can give
us information we need, not to get ourselves promoted."

"Really?" Mike asked. He seemed genuinely surprised.

The conference room door opened and Sergio came in. "Hey,
chief. I got another transcript for you." He handed a sheet of paper
to Patrón and poured himself some whiskey as he sat down at the
table. "What did I miss? Everyone looks down. What do we need?
Group hug? Group therapy? Group yoga?"

"Cultivated crop security in the southwest region," said Mike.

"What fucking security in the southwest fuck what?"

Patrón cut him off. "This was a second call? After the hospital?"

"That's right, *jefe*. Reis called Evorez directly at the Presidential
Palace. So once at the hospital during the noncoup, and once at
the palace to congratulate him and offer his assistance spreading
the revolution up north."

"This is from the ECHO program?"

Sergio nodded and looked at Victor, who took another swig
of Johnnie Walker.

"Guayandes seems on the verge of being taken over by the FRPT,
willingly," Patrón said. "We're quickly heading toward failed state
status here. I don't need to explain to any of you how serious that

is for US security. It'll be up to us to stop it." He grabbed his cup and stood up.

"Mike, you will be the key to this whole thing working." Mike looked elated. The others stayed silent. "Concentrate on cultivated crop security in the southwest region. Report the hell out of it. Everything. I want ten reports a month and several recruitments. We're counting on you."

Everyone left the conference room, except Mike, who stayed at the table taking in the enormous responsibility he had just been handed and looking ecstatic as he calculated when his next promotion might come.

"Chief," Victor pulled Patrón aside in the hallway. "Really? Cultivated crop security?"

"Mike was right about one thing, Victor. Director wants numbers. Director wants to see a lot of process so they can say we are busy. In Iraq, Mike had his interpreters translate local news stories that he then submitted as reports, driving up the station's metrics. Director loved being able to tell Congress how productive the Agency was over there. Let Mike check those boxes for us. That will keep Director from hounding us for reports. Mike is so excited, he'll meet Director's quota on his own." He patted Victor on the shoulder as he turned toward his corner office. "That will leave you guys free to actually do your job."

CHAPTER ELEVEN

Victor followed Patrón into the embassy's secure conference room, a small, stuffy space whose table was too big. Already seated on the far side was Laura Pillar, the embassy's chief political officer. A career diplomat who had spent the last fifteen years moving up in embassies around the world, one of her main jobs in Guayandes was to keep a straight face when El Toro's advisers fed her bullshit, as they had after a recent municipal election, saying the extra box of election ballots was only an error on paper and the vote tally of 512 voters—in a village of 304 people—was correct. Because Washington had been dragging its feet to replace the ambassador's deputy, who had left because he caught his wife having an affair with one of the Marines who guarded the embassy, Laura was officially second in the line of command after the ambassador and kept the daily operations of the embassy going.

She was watching a small TV in the corner of the room. It was live coverage of that day's *corrida*. The stadium was full and Victor saw the bull raging and running wild-eyed around the arena. The camera panned to the matador, who was dressed in the traditional *traje de luces*. Rather than being red or bright pink or orange, however, the matador's costume was a giant American flag, with stars across his blue back and red and white stripes across his front and down his legs.

He danced around the bull, taunting it. He stood on his tiptoes, his arms spread wide, an imposing figure in stars and stripes, rising before the bull. The bull snorted. The matador flung a red cape in front of the bull, teasing the beast, intimidating it, before picking it with *banderillas*. The masterful matador was bending the bull to his will.

The mighty bull resisted, however. His nostrils flared, wet snot flinging out, and his eyes bored into the matador. The bull breathed harder and louder, a look of determination crossing his dark face. He stared down the man who was attempting to overpower him. He snorted again. The stadium was hushed. The bull lifted his front left foot and scraped the ground with it, once, twice, before he rushed the matador, gouging him in the side. The matador doubled over, grasping at the bloody wound. The bull attacked again, slicing into the matador's thigh. He began to stumble. The bull attacked again, tossing the red-white-and-blue-clad matador up and nearly trampling him upon his landing.

Despite his efforts and his weapons, the matador had become a withering, quaking heap on the ground. The Star Spangled Banner was supine before the angry, raging bull.

The spectators cheered and the camera turned to Evorez. The president stood up in his tribunal and the arena went silent, except for the bull's heavy, wet breathing. Evorez put his arm out in front of him. The crowd in the arena was watching him expectantly. He looked left, then right, and turned his thumb down in a dramatic gesture. Six guards in green, blue, and red uniforms marched out and dragged the matador in his American flag suit through the dirt and out of the arena, leaving a trail of blood. The bull ran free across the sand. The bull had defeated the mighty matador. The arena erupted.

Laura clicked the television off.

Victor sat in a chair against the wall, as far from the table and the principals as he could. For one thing, he hated any and all meetings, especially with anyone based in Washington. For another, Victor did not want to attract attention from the ambassador.

He had met Ambassador Joyce Jones only twice, both times during receptions at her official residence. His first week in Guayandes, he had gone to a cocktail party there with Simon, who had warned Victor that Ambassador Jones loved her dog, a Pomeranian.

"I'm not exaggerating," Simon said as they pulled up to the residence's large iron gate. "She really loves her dog, so be nice to it if you want to win points."

They entered the residence and stopped in the grand foyer, a large rotunda with high ceilings and enormous vases of flowers placed in various recesses in the walls. Displayed in the middle of the room, as the central attraction, was a marble statue of a Pomeranian, curled up and asleep in a diamond-encrusted bed. On the wall hung a giant painting of a golden Pomeranian against a pink background and surrounded by an elaborate gilded frame.

"Joo see?" Simon said.

"Dude, why do you pronounce it like that?"

"I'm Puerto Rican."

"You're from Des Moines!"

Simon waved him off. "The monster dog has a lot of energy. I swear, that little ball of fur must be drinking espressos all day."

They walked through the house and out to the garden. The lush lawn spread out and down a hill, framed by pink and orange bougainvillea. Ambassador Jones stood on a stone terrace, receiving guests. Simon walked down the hill and straight to the bar. Victor got in the receiving line.

Slowly the guests moved forward, new arrivals in town paying their respects and presenting themselves to the US ambassador. Victor admired the view on Paxico volcano. He heard a yapping sound. He looked down the hill. Simon was under a tent and pointing at the Pomeranian, which was chasing a flower petal and barking uncontrollably. The dog made short, quick movements, causing the otherwise immobile petal to jump, setting the dog off on another chaotic tirade. Simon looked up at Victor and mouthed, "Joo see?"

The line moved forward. Victor took a deep breath and straightened his tie and jacket. It was his turn. He looked down at the tent again. The excited dog was trying to hump Simon's leg. Simon was pushing it away with his foot, saying "Choo! Choo!"

Chest up, shoulders back, Victor stepped forward to make the ambassador's acquaintance. As his foot came down, he felt something soft and squishy. Before he could jump back, he heard an enormous, "YAP!" He looked down to see he had stepped on the ambassador's prized Pomeranian. The tiny ball of fur gave him the most evil eye Victor had ever seen, before whimpering off to a corner. Victor looked back up. He was face to face with the ambassador. She did not look amused.

"How much money has the US government spent on training you to be observant?" Vanessa had asked, when he told her about the incident.

His second encounter with Ambassador Jones had come a few weeks later, when Vanessa and Oliver had first joined him in Guayandes. The ambassador was hosting a circus-themed welcome party for new families, including children, who got to jump in a bouncy house inflated on the lawn and eat hot dogs handed out by Uncle Sam on stilts.

The three of them had entered, Victor sure to lead Vanessa through the foyer so she could see the statue and portrait of the dog—"This is disturbing," Vanessa had said—and walked out to the terrace. The dog had come running to Oliver, sniffing his knees and yapping for attention. Oliver leaned down to pet the ball of fur and said, "Daddy! Is this the dog you stepped on?"

Ambassador Jones was standing right there.

Of course, the ambassador was a top diplomat. She handled such incidents with panache, immediately making people feel at ease, despite any faux pas. Still, Victor preferred not to attract her attention now, and so tried to blend into the conference room wall as she entered.

She was a petite woman with a good helmet of hair and it was clear, despite her size, she was a force to be reckoned with. She turned to Victor, low in his seat, and said, "It's nice to see you, Mr. Caro. How is your son?"

Victor started to gurgle something unintelligible but decided only to smile. She slid into the chair at the head of the table. Laura switched on a much larger television monitor perched on the wall. A timer icon swirled before there appeared a close up of Thomas Valencia, the assistant secretary of state for Latin America, who was based at the main State Department in Washington. The shot was a little too close up. The camera was pointing directly up Valencia's nostrils as he fiddled with a wire. As soon as he realized his nose hairs were filling a 52-inch screen viewed by his colleagues, he cleared his throat, settled the camera on the desk where he was, and leaned back to better place himself in view.

"*Hola*, comrades," he said to the room.

Valencia had been born and raised in Colorado, the son of two Tamindoan immigrants. Nominally, he held the culture close, but in reality he had only been to Tamindo once, on spring break in college. When he was nominated for the State Department position, the White House told the Senate Valencia's "essential skills" included his ability to find Tamindo on a map—this impressed the Senate—and "conversational Spanish." His most essential skill, however, was his ability to bundle donor money for the president's reelection campaign. This made him more essential than many of the career diplomats who had spent thirty years working the region. His ethnic-sounding name didn't hurt.

Because he had never actually experienced the true nature of "*¡Revolución!*" Valencia had fallen in love with the romantic notion of it. Victor had heard stories of Valencia wearing a beret and waxing poetic about leftist ideology and motorcycle rides across the continent while sipping Cava sparkling wine and eating aged Manchego cheese at parties. "I feel such indignation, comrade, when I see the world's injustices. Capitalism has made second-class citizens of most of the world's people," he once told a reporter from *Washingtonian* magazine who had interviewed him at a trendy *taqueria* near Washington's Logan Circle. The violent realities of *Revolución*—the disappearances and extra-judicial killings, for example—escaped him. He had a reputation for being sympathetic to Evorez and his notions of populism, while ignoring his poor stewardship of the economy and subsequent blaming of the United States for Guayandes' plight. He had become that which every US Foreign Service officer in the world hopes to avoid: the US diplomat who represents a foreign country to the United States, rather than the other way around.

Because the president and the secretary of state had other, more pressing priorities—war in the Middle East, nuclear proliferation, terrorism, Middle Eastern nuclear terrorism—Valencia was free to rule his Latin American fiefdom from Washington as he pleased. This corner of the earth was insignificant enough that it received no White House-level interest, but significant enough that, if ignored completely, it could cause long-term headaches for the United States, mostly because of drugs and immigration.

While this was exactly the combination that made it a paradise for case officers like Victor—interesting challenges and issues that actually mattered, combined with little interference from Washington—it was also the kind of environment in which a weenie like Valencia could hold an outsized influence over policy.

"Hello, Thomas." Ambassador Jones's voice was low and restrained. Victor wondered if that was contempt he heard in her undertones.

"I've just spoken with Rafa," Valencia said. "I was very relieved to hear he is safe and recovering. What a nightmare that must have been for him." Victor noted that Valencia used the first name of the president of Guayandes.

"We're all safe and accounted for here at the embassy," Ambassador Jones said. "Thanks for asking."

Valencia either didn't catch the insult or chose to ignore it and he jumped into an excited description of the flowers he planned to send to El Toro. "Red roses, of course, and some hydrangea, to add a splash of blue, and some leaves for the green. So we have all the colors of the Guayandan flag. I think Rafa will appreciate that. I've been composing a poem, as well. 'The mountains of Guayandes are tall and mighty, its sea is clear and blue. But from east to west and north to south, no president compares to—'"

Ambassador Jones cut him off. "Thomas, we've been rather busy down here the last few days, trying to sort out exactly what happened."

"What *happened*? Rafa survived a coup, that's what happened. The police tried to oust him, but the military stayed loyal."

"It isn't quite as clear cut as that," said Jones. "Laura?"

Laura picked up her notes but didn't look at them. "I've spoken with Foreign Minister Flores. He told me the government believes the police were provoked into action after being indoctrinated by American police films." Laura said.

Victor stifled a laugh and hoped he was out of range for the camera so Valencia couldn't see his reaction. Laura glanced at him and bit her lip. She had to at least pretend she took her host country's government seriously.

Ambassador Jones said, "Trevor, why don't you share what information you have?"

Victor wondered for a moment who Trevor was, then realized she meant Patrón. Despite having known him for more than a decade, Victor wasn't sure he had ever heard his true name spoken out loud.

Patrón took a sip of his coffee. His white moustache was stained yellow from an earlier cup. He had no papers in front of him. He nodded to the ambassador and turned to the camera and Valencia.

"We have confirmed that this was not a coup but rather was an orchestrated attempt on the part of President Evorez—*Rafa*—to solidify his ranks and consolidate his power. He plans to use the event as well to sack the chief of police tomorrow."

"Police Chief del Campo is one of the more moderate officials still around," said Laura.

"Not for long," Patrón said. "Additionally, *Rafa*," he glanced at Valencia, "is being aided in his efforts by the FRPT."

"What are you insinuating?" Valencia stammered.

"There's no insinuation. I'm telling you in a very straightforward manner that Evorez wants to be a dictator and the FRPT is helping him." He stared at Valencia staring down at him from the giant screen. "Guayandes is going from petro-state to narco-state. Fast."

"It's preposterous what you say. I just spoke with Rafa directly. Who is your source?"

"First of all," Patrón leaned back in his chair, a picture of calm. "I wouldn't trust Evorez to be the most forthcoming with you on this issue. Second, we have several sources telling us the same thing.

In my business, we call that corroboration. Third, no fucking way I'm telling you my sources."

Victor could see Valencia's face turning red. Valencia looked at the ambassador. Laura looked down at her notes. Victor pushed as far against the wall as he could.

"I would wait on the flowers, Thomas," Ambassador Jones said. "And hold off on the poem."

Valencia glared down at them. The screen went black as he cut the line.

CHAPTER TWELVE

Adam walked into the university cafeteria, a glassed-in box off the main atrium, and stood awkwardly on the side, scanning the tables. His backpack was slung over one shoulder. He had shaved that morning, giving him a baby-faced look.

A young woman in ripped jeans, burgundy Converse Chuck Taylors, and a black Pitbull T-shirt approached him. "Adam?"

"Valentina? I wasn't sure how I would find you," he said in Spanish.

"You were easy to spot. Shall we sit?"

Valentina Orellana was an international relations student at the Universidad de Guayandes. She came from a middle-class Guayita family, wealthy enough to go to college but not to travel to Miami regularly. She had posted signs around the university's foreign students dorm, offering Spanish conversation sessions for a small remuneration.

Although Adam had been able to follow Victor's conversation with Fernandez at the volcano, he knew he needed to improve his Spanish skills. He had observed how much better Victor,

Wes, Simon, Sergio, and Patrón understood how Guayandes and Guayandans worked because they understood and spoke the language. Mike, on the other hand, was chasing wheat or god knows what and relying on Director to help with translations.

Adam had found Valentina's advertisement and researched her. She was involved in the university's Model United Nations team and was active in the student union. Furthermore, he had seen on her Facebook page that her father was a military pilot. She'd likely provide interesting conversation and insight into the thinking of the young generation and, perhaps, the Guayandan military, all while improving Adam's Spanish.

They found a somewhat clean table and sat down. A nearby television was showing highlights from the bullfight, replaying the scene of the matador surrendering to the bull. Adam pulled a banana out of his backpack and offered half to Valentina. She looked at him funny and shook her head.

"Where are you from, Adam? How did you end up in Guayandes?"

Adam launched into his cover story, which he had prepared anticipating these very questions. "I'm from Idaho, but I studied in Washington, DC. I'm working at the embassy here, in the political section. They do it to introduce young professionals to the Foreign Service, to try to attract new Foreign Service officers." As Adam recited this, he realized he had forgotten to mention any of this to Laura and made a mental note to do so when he returned to the embassy later that afternoon. He felt a little bad, but he had seen too many examples where it had been better to ask for forgiveness than permission. She'd understand.

"You are a diplomat?"

"I'm learning about being a diplomat."

"I want to be a diplomat," Valentina said. "I would love to go to New York and represent my country at the United Nations."

Suddenly, the cafeteria went dark. A hush fell over the room. Adam heard a refrigerator vibrate and moan before it went silent. The electricity had gone out.

Valentina let out a frustrated sigh. "It's happening more often, have you noticed?"

Another student came over to their table and said to Valentina, "What is this shit? This is the third blackout this week! Did you talk to the university maintenance staff like we discussed at the last meeting?"

"The student union prepared a memo for the head of the university," said Valentina. "I personally spoke with the engineers. They haven't done maintenance on the system for years. The government is supposed to give money for maintenance, and they don't. They budget it, put it on paper, but never actually give it. It's the same story across the grid."

Valentina's friend went back to her table. Valentina gave Adam an apologetic look. "As I was saying, I want to represent my country, but I'm not sure I want to represent Evorez. His economic policies are going to hurt us in the long run. This ridiculous move firing everyone at Guayandes Petroleum is only the latest example. You see us here? We can't keep the lights on. Guayandes has less oil because we have no one who knows how to find it or get it out of the ground. Now we have nothing to sell and no way to get cash. The money for maintenance never arrives, and you and I sit here in the dark."

The electricity came back on. The refrigerator shook to life. The television flickered. President Evorez was speaking.

"We are working to restore electricity across the city. It has come back in some pockets, I understand, but we will restore it everywhere. Let me be clear," he looked straight at the camera, "this is yet another example of the imperialist swine trying to sabotage us, another attempt to interfere in our elections. We will not stand for this! We will not allow our sovereignty to be sabotaged!"

Valentina looked at Adam. "You see what I mean? My dad told me that since the coup, Evorez and that Espina adviser of his have been scheming against the people." She caught herself and looked nervous. "I probably shouldn't say those things. My dad is in the military. I don't want to get him in trouble."

"Who am I going to tell?" Adam said innocently. "I thought the military supported Evorez?"

"Generally, yes, they've stayed loyal, as an organization. The military is made up of individuals, though, and they are all human and think for themselves. Well, some of them do, at least."

"What does your dad do in the military?"

"He's a pilot."

"I thought Evorez had dismembered much of the Air Force."

"What?"

"Taken apart," Adam said.

"*Dismantled!*" Valentina corrected Adam's Spanish. "Dismantled the Air Force. Yes. I was afraid you thought he had chopped the pilots to pieces. We are not savages here."

Adam laughed.

Valentina continued, "Yes, he dismantled most of the Air Force, but he kept a handful of pilots, not for combat, but for flying him and Espina around the country. My dad is a chauffeur in the sky. The coming months will be busy for him, as Evorez campaigns throughout the country. In any case," she glanced at the television, where Evorez was still talking, "let's hope the lights stay on and my father stays in one piece."

She changed the subject, and Adam let her. For the next hour, they discussed movies and music and art. Valentina would correct Adam every now and then, or help him find a word he didn't know. Occasionally, she taught him a slang phrase or a bad word.

At the end of their session, as Adam was packing up his pen and notebook, Valentina said, shyly, "About my payment . . ."

"Of course!" Adam replied. He reached in his backpack for his wallet.

Valentina glanced around the cafeteria and leaned in toward Adam. "I was wondering if you'd be willing to pay me in dollars, instead of chavis." She looked around again to make sure no one had heard her.

"That's not a problem at all," Adam said. He handed her a twenty-dollar bill. She tucked it in her pocket.

"I appreciate that." She grabbed her bag off the other seat. "Same time next week?"

"That works fine," he said.

Valentina leaned over and gave Adam kisses on either cheek. She smiled. *"Adiós,* Adam." She turned and walked away.

CHAPTER THIRTEEN

Vanessa woke to the sound of Victor cussing. That wasn't unusual, but the fervor and volume made her think that this time, something might really be wrong. She wrapped herself in a fleece sweatshirt against the morning chill and stepped out of the dark bedroom into the bright light of morning shining in through their duplex windows. Victor was stomping around the living room looking like he was about to throw his laptop through the window. She went downstairs and pried the laptop from his grip. "What's happened?"

"There's a leak."

"I'll call a plumber. You don't need to get so worked up."

"No, a *leaker*. Someone is leaking secrets. Look." He pointed to the laptop, which was open to the *New York News*. Vanessa read the story.

```
The Whistleblower Who Came In From The Cold:
Intelligence Community Contractor Absconds With
Classified Documents And Shares Them In The
Name Of Public Good
```

Intelligence Community contractor Lawrence Blackhouse has blown the whistle on top secret US intelligence programs that monitored the phone calls and electronic communications of hundreds of thousands of people.

"US government surveillance of its own citizens has reached Orwellian proportions," Blackhouse said in an exclusive interview from an undisclosed location in China, where he went with the millions of US government classified documents. "I'm looking to highlight government overreach and oppression of its citizens. I am here in China with these documents to do just that. The US government today could be compared to authoritarian regimes of yesteryear. I hope the Chinese government will be amenable to helping me spread that message."

"Sounds like he hasn't read much about China's government," said Vanessa. She continued reading.

"The American people need to understand their own government is collecting information on them," Blackhouse said. "That is why I have handed over these documents to a transparency organization. The Committee for Clear and Candid Policy will release these documents on their website at CCCP.org."

Vanessa looked at Victor. He was staring out the window.

Blackhouse told the *News* he also has information about US intelligence efforts against China. Although he did not elaborate about how exposing US spying operations against China achieved his stated goal of exposing US surveillance operations against Americans, he did say, "This is about transparency. I'm a humble servant of the American people, looking to highlight criminality by our own government."

The US government has frozen Blackhouse's bank accounts. When asked who was paying for his living expenses and his legal representation, he refused to answer.

"Transparency for thee, but not for me," Vanessa said. She continued.

The trove of documents also revealed the National Security Agency has been listening in on the personal phone calls of several heads of state. In one example Blackhouse provided, again saying it was for the protection of the American people, documents revealed the US intelligence community had collected recordings of the personal phone calls of Guayandan President Rafael Evorez. He also revealed that the NSA had compromised that country's mobile phone and internet provider, Kapokom.

Vanessa looked at Victor. "Oh, fuck."
"Keep reading," he said.

> The documents reveal that US intelligence agencies
> have been listening in on phone conversations of
> leaders of the Revolutionary Armed Forces for the
> Liberation of the Formerly Free Peoples of Tamindo,
> the FRPT.

Vanessa shut the laptop and turned to Victor. "How fucked are you?"

He took a long, deep breath and let it out with a huff. "Really fucked."

***

Laura slipped into the deep leather seats of the armored Cadillac and signaled the driver to go. They exited the embassy compound through several layers of security, a guard finally opening the last gate that allowed the car out onto the city streets. The Guayandan minister of foreign affairs had called her at home early in the morning to summon her to a meeting, the topic of which he hadn't cared to elaborate on over the phone. The fact that he had called personally, rather than having his secretary do it, put Laura on alert and she showered and dressed quickly to give herself a chance to get to the embassy to figure out what could be wrong. The ambassador, along with her dog, was away, dedicating a new school that had been built with US funds in a rural village in the south. One look at the news and Laura had known it was going to be a complicated day that would test her diplomacy skills.

She had called Patrón. "Get ready for the worst," he had said. Were those Jacuzzi bubbles she was hearing in the background?

He hung up as a woman's voice in the background said, "Come in, Papi! The water is warm!"

As the car approached the main ministry, Laura instructed her driver to bring her around to a side entrance she normally used, but the ministry's security guards directed the car back to the main entrance and Laura realized the minister wanted to make a public spectacle of her, almost certainly at the request of El Toro himself.

She stepped out of the car and into a sea of local reporters. She had developed a good rapport with the media over her time in Guayandes. They had recorded many of the development projects the embassy had helped with and generally had a favorable view of her, the ambassador, and the embassy, since such projects affected them and their families personally. She saw one reporter who had interviewed her and written a glowing article about a new health facility in a nearby town. He asked her, "Is it true?" adding quickly, "I'm sorry. I have to ask. It's my job."

She pushed through the crowd and into the building, a colonial era remnant that was pink and lined with porticoes. The minister's personal assistant was waiting in the lobby. He was a short man in a dark striped suit with a big smile on his face.

"The minister is waiting for you."

Laura followed him down the hallway and into an elevator that opened into an executive suite. A large oil painting portrait of Evorez—smiling, dressed in an indigenous shirt, and staring into the middle distance—lined an entire wall. Heavy red velvet curtains adorned the gilded frame. A well-dressed secretary sat at a large oak desk opposite the painting, staring at it, longingly. The minister's assistant snapped at the secretary as he led Laura to two elaborately carved wooden doors. He knocked, opened one, and ushered Laura into the office of the Guayandan minister of foreign affairs.

Minister Santos Flores sat behind a leather-top desk strewn with small brass statues of various birds and neat, small piles of papers. He did not stand or shake her hand, but rather motioned for Laura to sit down across from him. As she did so, he sat quietly with his fingers interlaced on his desk over a single official envelope. Once Laura was seated, he handed her the envelope, made eye contact for four seconds, and then looked to his assistant, motioning him to lead Laura out.

The assistant led her past the enamored secretary and into the elevator, where he escorted her down and out through the media pool to her waiting Cadillac. He helped her into the car and closed the door. All without a word.

Laura fingered the envelope as the car pulled away. She didn't need to look at it. The reception she had received had already told her what the letter certainly said. Once she opened it, it would become part of the official record and she wasn't ready for that. The ambassador loved Guayandes, almost as much as she loved her dog.

Three blocks before the embassy, Laura opened the letter, which confirmed her fear: "Due to the revelations about the United States government's illegal spying in the Republic of Guayandes, the President of the Republic, the Great and Honorable Rafael Evorez, has classified United States Ambassador Joyce Jones *Persona Non Grata* and requests she exit the country within seventy-two hours."

It was official. The ambassador had to leave. Laura would be in charge of the embassy.

***

Victor went into the Men's Locker Room. The Reggaeton group Chino y Nacho was playing. He walked over to the CD player and yanked the cord out of the wall. He heard Wes deep inside the cubicle farm. "What the fuck, man?" Victor walked into his office and slumped in his chair.

He picked up his bowl of potpourri and inhaled while he stared at the kill list poster, Reis and his cigar sitting at the top of the pyramid, no red X over the picture. Wes appeared at his door.

"Seriously, dude. What the fuck?"

Victor shook the potpourri bowl to release some of the aroma. Wes leaned over and took it from him. He took a big whiff and his face relaxed. "That's actually very soothing." He inhaled again then handed the bowl back to Victor, who took another smell.

"For years, we've been working on decapitating the FRPT," Victor said. "We set up ECHO to help get location information on their leaders. We then hand that information to the Tamindo military and they do the dirty work. What do we do without ECHO?" He looked at Wes. "These Blackhouse leaks could be lethal for us, both literally and figuratively. That's going to mean more frequent trips into the jungle for us, at a time when more FRPT militants are feeling cozy and at home here in Guayandes. Our chances of getting kidnapped or killed just went up. And the whole operation against the FRPT is at risk if no one can get the information."

He looked at a map of Guayandes and Tamindo on his wall. "And why? Why are they coming over the border? What are they doing up there? So many people in such a short amount of time. Are they scattering in the jungle up there? Or are they planning to make Guayandes their headquarters?"

Simon came into Victor's office. "Did you guys hear the news?" He spotted the bowl of potpourri. "What's this?" He grabbed it and took a deep breath. "That's really nice."

"That Lawrence Blackhouse is a douchebag? Yes, we heard that," said Wes.

Simon handed the bowl back to Victor. "No, the chief of police. Evorez sacked him this morning. Say goodbye to any law and order that was left in this country."

The main door of the Men's Locker Room buzzed. Simon went out and returned with Laura.

"Do you guys know when Patrón will be in?" she asked. "Nice potpourri. The lavender color fits nicely in this room. I need to let him know the ambassador has been PNG'ed."

"Today keeps getting better," Victor said. "Anyone want whiskey? If I'm going to spend the next twenty-eight years in an FRPT camp in the middle of the Amazon, I'd better enjoy the finer things in life now."

Simon went out for a second and then returned.

"There's none left in the conference room."

"Really, this is the perfect fucking day," Victor said.

They heard the main door of the office open and close. Laura leaned out to look. "We're in here."

Andy appeared at Victor's door carrying a box. "Why so glum?"

Victor and the others shook their heads, too defeated to speak.

Andy hoisted the box up a little. "I've got booze. Will that help?"

"As always, Andy, your timing is impeccable."

"I'm a support officer, Victor. I support my officers. Cheers."

CHAPTER FOURTEEN

Oliver's backpack was a raggedy mess, papers popping out of open pockets, crumbs floating around inside, and grass stains streaking the outside. Vanessa pulled out the papers and the remnants of yesterday's lunch. She ruffled through the papers, glancing at a memorandum reminding parents about this weekend's Global Leaders Summit, which was meant to "bring together future potential Global Leaders who will lead the world in convictions!" *They must mean they will have strong convictions,* Vanessa thought. *Although these days, who knows?* She took out a note from the gym teacher reminding students to wear a "gym suite and snickers" to class. It was an American school, but most of the administrative employees were local Guayandans. Some things got lost in translation. She packed Oliver's lunch and loaded him on the school bus.

The house was unpacked. She had a car and had found the fastest routes to the priority spots, including the grocery, the embassy, and the best place in town for margaritas. The kid was adjusted and happy. Vanessa was ready to start focusing on herself. She shed her jeans and sneakers for a skirt and flats and headed to the embassy.

As she walked around the compound toward the chancery entrance, she saw Ellie, nearly crumbling beneath a pile of boxes she was carrying toward the facilities management building, where the embassy stored refrigerators, washers and dryers, and other household appliances for the residences of the American staff. Vanessa plucked the top box from the pile in Ellie's arms, as Ellie chirped, "Hey, *chica*!"

"What are you doing with all these?"

"We got a pouch full of replacement parts. I'm bringing them over to the warehouse."

"Why are *you* bringing them?"

"They're a little understaffed right now, since Rachel is on maternity leave. I'm helping out."

"Who is Rachel?"

"You know Rachel."

"I don't recall meeting a Rachel." Ellie had a penchant for knowing everyone in the embassy community and insisting everyone else must know them, too.

"You know her. She's the one who talked about her wooden duck decoy collection at Lunch Bunch that one time."

"I think I would remember that."

"You know her." Ellie spotted one of the facilities management local employees exiting the warehouse. "Jorge! Hi, Jorge! Can you help us please? These boxes are *muy* heavy." The employee came over and took the boxes from Ellie and Vanessa. He smiled and nodded as Ellie said, "Thank you! Thank you!"

"You know you could say *gracias* instead," Vanessa pointed out.

"He understands. Right, Jorge?"

He nodded and smiled again and turned to take the boxes to the warehouse.

"Is his name Jorge?" Vanessa asked.

"At some point, I'll be right," Ellie said. "I gotta run. I have *mucho* things to do before we go to Lunch Bunch."

"I'm not going to Lunch . . ."

Ellie had already gone into the warehouse and was yelling, "Jorge! Wait for me!"

Vanessa entered the chancery, waving at the Marine security guard on duty who had given Oliver a tour of the embassy's weapons systems and let the child wear his helmet. She went upstairs, wound her way through a cubicle farm, and knocked on the open door of the head of human resources.

Gloria Wilson was playing Solitaire on her computer and didn't bother to click it closed when she greeted Vanessa and told her to have a seat. She had long gray hair and a friendly face. She had tacked various papers to a corkboard above her desk. Vanessa saw a pay date calendar and several thick packets of regulations, including one that read, "Amendment to FAM-132-2014: On the Recycle of Household Furniture Pieces For Use in Official Residential Non-Commercial Spaces of More than 519 Square Footage Measurement."

"What can I help you with today?" she asked.

"I'm looking for some guidance on getting a job here," Vanessa said. "I've taken leave from the FBI, where I was a manager, but I know that office has no positions here. I thought there might be some opportunities to help out elsewhere in the embassy."

"You have great timing," Gloria said. She dug through some papers on her desk and pulled out a single sheet.

Vanessa felt excited. A new opportunity. A new adventure!

"The Consular office is looking for a receptionist," the woman said. Vanessa bit her tongue. The woman looked through another pile and said, "Aha!" as she pulled out a second piece of paper. "And the medical unit needs a part-time scheduler." She looked at Vanessa, who tried to smile.

"Did I mention I was a manager at the FBI?"

"You did."

"I was thinking more along the lines of the security office or Drug Enforcement Administration or something."

"Those jobs aren't for wives."

"I'm disqualified because I'm a wife?"

"Those are jobs for people coming from Washington," Gloria explained.

"I just arrived from Washington."

"Which means you are already here."

"I can't do the job here because I am already here?"

"Exactly."

"Isn't it good that I'm already here? It's one less person the government has to spend money on to get here and to house and everything."

"Wives aren't qualified for those jobs."

"I'm sorry," Vanessa said, leaning forward. "I'm not following. What does this have to do with being a wife?"

"You're right, I should have been clearer. Those are not EFM jobs."

"EFM? Is that an eighties band?"

"Eligible Family Member. EFM. Also known as a dependent. Those jobs are not for dependents. Most dependents are wives."

"I'm a dependent wife? So I can't get a job?" *Or I can't get a job, which will* make *me a dependent wife*, she thought. *Oh, dear god.*

"Of course you can get a job. We also have an opening in the mailroom sorting packages."

Vanessa glared at her.

"I'm getting the sense maybe you'd like something with a little more substance?" Gloria asked.

Vanessa nodded.

Gloria brandished another sheet of paper. "Here we go. I think this will be more up your alley. The US Agency for International Development."

Vanessa perked up. She had no background in economic development, projects like building schools and wells, but at least it was interesting work, work that might even help people every now and then. "Great, Gloria. Thank you. Tell me about that opening."

"They need a note taker at their weekly staff meeting. It's a GS-6 position."

"I'm a GS-14."

Gloria looked up from the paper at Vanessa. "Fancy." She placed the job description in front of Vanessa. "If you're interested, we should get started now. There's quite a bit of paperwork involved and it might take about a year to clear you for the position."

"I'll be more than halfway through our tour, probably already preparing for the next move."

"Great! We have you occupied until you're scheduled to leave!"

Vanessa took a deep breath and summoned all her patience. "How about on the local economy? What options do I have for working outside the embassy?"

"We don't encourage that. It's a very difficult process, very lengthy."

"What exactly is involved?"

"We don't know. That's the problem. President Evorez is constantly changing the regulations. He's always issuing new bureaucratic rulings that require pushing more paper. It's quite tiring."

Vanessa wondered if Gloria understood the irony in what she was saying.

"Here," Gloria said, sitting upright suddenly and turning with purpose to her computer. She minimized her Solitaire game and clicked through a number of documents before hitting "print" on one of them. "I really want to help you. I'm printing out the Bilateral Treaty on Local Economy Employment Reciprocation. It lists the types of industries dependents are allowed to work in and outlines the process for getting a tax identification number and other necessary documents. It's everything you need to know about the process."

"Thanks," Vanessa said. "I appreciate it."

"The printer is out there by the hallway. Thanks for coming by and so glad I could help."

Vanessa exited the office. She could hear the printer, buried between rows of cubicles, and made her way toward the sound, stopping in her tracks when she saw the machine. Papers were strewn all over the floor, hundreds of them, and the printer was still spitting out more of the Bilateral Treaty on Local Economy Employment Reciprocation. She watched it print page 246, which had the words "as amended, per ref 266 of FAR-8900662 under the codification of Superior Act . . ." Vanessa turned on her heels and walked out.

She pushed open the stairwell door and then ran. She ran down the stairs, trying not to hyperventilate, and raced around the corner toward the exit. As she pushed the door open, Savannah came in and nearly knocked Vanessa over with her aura of enthusiasm.

"Hiyeeeeee!" she burst out as she hugged Vanessa. She wore enormous gold bangles that clanged as she moved, and she was chewing and snapping gum. Loudly. "It's so good to see you here! I was going to call you! You *have* to come to Lunch Bunch today. *Have* to!" Vanessa tried to speak, but Savannah wouldn't let her get a word out. "I won't hear any of it. You simply *have* to be there. Jane will be speaking. Isn't that exciting? She's a life coach! I know we can all use a little of that in our lives! Am I right?"

Vanessa pushed past her and ran outside, as though escaping a kidnapper. When she felt she had reached freedom, she slowed down to catch her breath and collect herself. Standing in the middle of the pathway, she stared out at Paxico volcano, rising majestically in the distance under a clear blue sky. *How did I get here?*

"Good day?"

Vanessa snapped back to the here and now and turned to see Victor standing to the side, smoking a cigarette.

"I no longer have a job with the government, but somehow the bureaucracy is still crushing me. I can't get a job here because I'm already here. Now I'm supposed to have lunch with an overly enthusiastic southern belle wannabe and a life coach."

"Just don't find God, please. I'd prefer if we could keep our spiritual crises secular."

"You?" she asked.

"Trying to figure out how to break a massive narco-terror group that's possibly funding this country's president, who just kicked out our ambassador, by the way, after this idiot Blackhouse blew my covert action program in the name of fucking transparency."

"I think my Lunch Bunch is more important."

"It is," he agreed.

"I'll be growing emotionally with my life coach and, I don't know, knitting maybe?" she said.

"You're also raising a future Global Leader," Victor said.

"Making sure he has the proper snickers for school before getting convicted."

Victor put his arms around Vanessa. "We should have stayed in DC," he said.

She kissed him. "We're here. We're going to make it work."

"Look at you two lovebirds!" Victor and Vanessa pulled apart as Ellie approached them. "You ready?" she asked Ness. Without waiting for a reply, she turned to Victor and assured him, "She's ready." She grabbed Vanessa. "*¡Adiós!* We'll see you tonight at happy hour!"

Victor stumped out his cigarette as he watched Ellie drag his wife to meet her life coach.

***

"We could skip Lunch Bunch and go get margaritas instead," Vanessa said, as Ellie made a six-point turn to get her minivan out of its parking space.

"This is your community now. You need to make an effort to be nice," Ellie replied. "I love you and I love hanging out with you, but you need to expand your social circle."

"Yes, Mom."

They drove onto the busy streets and stopped at a red light. It turned green.

"Wait! Don't go yet!" Vanessa yelled. She rolled down her window. She motioned to a woman standing in the intersection. She was selling hammocks. "Over here!" Vanessa called.

"The light is green," Ellie said.

"Which do you prefer? The red one or the blue one?" Vanessa asked, looking through the stack of bright fabric and ropes. "How much?" she asked the woman.

"Still green," Ellie said.

"I don't see a green one. Red or blue? I think I like the blue. Five hundred chavis? How about three hundred chavis? Fine, three fifty." She took the blue hammock and closed her window.

"It's red," Ellie said.

"No, I got the blue one."

"The light is red. Any other shopping you want to finish before the light changes again?"

"I'm good. Thanks."

Ellie drove on. They came to another red light. A man with no hands approached the car, asking for money. Ellie grabbed her purse.

"What are you doing?" asked Vanessa.

"I'm going to give him a little money."

"You're only encouraging him. Every time you stop at this intersection, he'll expect more money."

"With that logic, you are going to own a lot of hammocks by the time you leave Guayandes."

"Maybe he doesn't really need the money. Maybe he's faking it."

"He has no hands, Ness." She dropped some change in a hat he was squeezing between his wrists. "Here you go, Jorge."

Ellie pulled into the neighborhood compound where her house was and parked outside the compound wall of the house itself. "I want to change into jeans before we go." The two of them went inside.

Ellie ran up the stairs to change and Vanessa went into the kitchen to wait. She peeked in the pantry. Ellie had stocked it floor to ceiling with juice boxes, canned goods, and boxes of macaroni and cheese, as well as twenty giant water bottles for the water machine. One entire shelf was lined with every kind of Cheerios known to mankind. Stacks of beer and wine filled another.

She looked at the photos stuck to the refrigerator, Ellie and Simon's kids at the park, in the pool, playing with the ambassador's dog. She saw another picture of her and Victor with Ellie and Simon at the base of Paxico volcano. They were all smiling. It was from a few weeks back, when the four of them had parked the kids with Ellie's nanny and hiked up the volcano, well onto the glacier. Up there, at more than 17,000 feet, Ellie had whipped out a thermos of hot coffee and offered it to all of them. The sky was a perfect blue and was clear as far as they could see down the alley of volcanoes that marked the fracturing continent. When they had finished their snack, they had each put their backpacks on their chests and sat down on their rain jackets and slid the entire way down. It had taken nearly three hours to climb up. They had made it back to the base in about ten minutes.

Vanessa sighed. She sometimes missed the satisfaction that came with the mission of her old job, but man, she loved these new adventures.

"I've got my cool jeans on, ready to go," Ellie said, entering the kitchen.

"If there's ever a major disaster in Guayita, I'm going to seek shelter in your pantry," said Vanessa.

"Bring your hammock. There's space in there to string it up." She grabbed a bottle of wine. "Let's go learn how to live."

Vanessa looked at the photo of them at the base of Paxico. "I think we're doing alright."

CHAPTER FIFTEEN

"Is she on the plane?" President Evorez brushed some crumbs off his nylon tracksuit. It made a *swish swish* sound.

"Ambassador Jones officially left Guayandan air space at eight-oh-three this morning," Segundo replied.

"And the dog?"

"Also gone."

Evorez stood up and circled around the desk. He looked up at a painted portrait of himself that he had recently commissioned. In it, he was adorned in a green, blue, and red poncho and was seated on the back of a fierce-looking bull. His arm and finger were outstretched, pointing to the lands he planned to conquer, although when the artist was painting it, Evorez had been pointing across the room to a small fishbowl with a goldfish in it.

"Was it too harsh?" Evorez asked.

"Hardly, Your Excellency," Segundo responded. "It is yet another forceful action to show you will not allow the imperialists to the north to gouge us anymore. The time of the shark is over. The minnows are rising up!"

"Some people liked her. She built a number of schools and hospitals. Will they blame me?"

"*You* built those schools and hospitals. The people can get confused. They do not know what they think. It is up to you to remind them."

The buzzer on Evorez's desk buzzed. "Thomas Valencia, of the United States Department of State," the secretary announced.

"Don't let him cower you," Segundo said to Evorez. "Remember, you are El Toro. Make him remember that, too."

Evorez clicked the speakerphone.

"It's too late to change my mind on this, Thomas."

"Change your mind, Rafa? What on earth for? I'm calling to apologize to *you*." Evorez and Segundo exchanged pleased expressions. "I am terribly embarrassed that our spies would stoop so low against such a great man. Lawrence Blackhouse has done us all a great favor. Maybe a little sunlight on America's own shortcomings will help curb our arrogance when dealing with others. This push for transparency is exactly what the United States needs. How disrespectful of our intelligence agencies, thinking they could *spy* on people. Seriously, who do they think they are?"

Segundo couldn't believe he was hearing this. Guayandes' own spy services were, of course, doing everything in their power to collect intelligence against the United States. Segundo had personally directed some of those operations. The American operation against a president who had, on numerous occasions, compared the United States to a foul-smelling porcine animal and blamed the country for all its ills was to be expected. The Blackhouse revelations provided a good opportunity for Evorez to score a political point, but

Segundo wasn't so naïve as to believe spies shouldn't spy. Where would the fun be in that?

Evorez stuttered for a response. Segundo looked hard at him and made a gesture of stabbing a knife. "Stay strong," he mouthed to the president.

"This is precisely why the dismissal of Ambassador Jones is only the first of many steps I have planned as a response to your spies' devious actions." Evorez looked to Segundo for approval. Segundo nodded. "I shall make a speech tonight to the great nation of Guayandes, explaining the treachery of the United States. Perhaps you will use this as an opportunity to address your own problems of transparency and government overreach."

"You could not be more right, Rafa," Valencia said. "We are turning ourselves into a police state. It is almost—it saddens me to say it, but someone has to—as if the United States were on its way to becoming an authoritarian state. Our security services are out of control. It's time we take a good, hard look at ourselves."

"You do that, Thomas. Perhaps these Blackhouse leaks will be good for you."

CHAPTER SIXTEEN

President Evorez adjusted his tricolor sash over his dark suit jacket. He did a few squats, grunting each time, to get his blood pumping. His popularity had risen steadily since the police demonstrations, which he had successfully framed as an attempted coup, and the police had duly fallen into line after he fired their chief. Meanwhile, the people of Guayandes had responded positively to his harsh response to the United States in the wake of the Blackhouse leaks. His base responded to the emotional messages best. Today, he planned to appeal to their emotions again, to solidify his grip on power and hold the opposition down. After all, he had an election coming up in a few months and the opposition party was beginning to agitate for change. His firing of half the workers at the state oil company had played well with his base, and provided many of them with well-paying jobs. Unfortunately, they had not been very successful in getting oil out of the ground, or in finding oil to begin with. That was all about to change. He would put on a good show to refocus them on what truly mattered: him.

A giant canvas unfurled behind the makeshift stage in the middle of the jungle, where the few qualified engineers left at Guayandes Petroleum had set up a rig for Evorez. The canvas showed a menacing black bull on a red background. TV cameras were set up all around. Segundo had made sure all the news shows would cover the event. The energy of the crowd built up as a group of drummers performed. People stamped their feet to the beat. Their anticipation grew as the drums got louder, their beats faster. The drums banged a climactic boom and the crowd exploded when El Toro stepped on stage.

He strutted in front of the crowd, letting them admire him.

"It is so kind of you to come out and see me!" he yelled to them.

Many people were still streaming off the buses Evorez's government had provided to bring them to the site, and which his police had encouraged many rural villagers to get on, lest they have difficulties later on.

The drumming began anew, as Evorez climbed up on a crane. At each level, he stopped to wave at the crowd. He reached the top and settled into the seat. The drumming was pulsing now. The crowd was stamping its feet in unison. Evorez placed his hand over a giant red button. He held it there a moment, allowing the excitement to build, and then he pushed the button dramatically, his eyes wide with anticipation. The drumming halted and the crowd went silent.

Nothing happened.

The drummers glanced at each other. The crowd murmured.

He pushed the button again. Then a few more times.

A second later, a giant fountain of oil erupted out of a hole in the ground, shooting forty, fifty feet in the air, raining oil down onto the jungle's canopy. The drummers went wild. The crowd cheered. Children threw confetti.

Evorez climbed down from the crane as the people applauded his unbelievable ability to find oil in the middle of nowhere.

"How did he do it?" someone in the crowd yelled.

"It's a miracle!" shouted another.

He returned to the stage. The people quieted down, waiting for him to speak.

"Sovereignty!" he yelled. The word echoed through the crowd as the sound carried to the speakers farther and farther back. The people cheered. Evorez knew that single word always got them worked up, even without context, so he yelled it again. "Sovereignty!" The crowd was now chanting the word.

"I can smell the malodorous stench of the swine from the north, trying to squash us under their ungulate feet, covered in feces and filth that they seek to spread to keep us down. They have used us for our oil, *our* natural resources. They have used us to enrich themselves. They are taking our sovereignty!" The crowd cheered again. "They infiltrated our mobile phone and internet company, threatening our sovereignty!" The people were getting really worked up now. "Then they spied on your president's phone conversations. They have come directly into the Presidential Palace! They accuse Guayandes of going from petro-state to narco-state. Yet they present no evidence. It is only lies. Lies to divide us. Lies! They are trampling on our sovereignty!" The crowd was in a frenzy now. Evorez lifted his chin, surveyed the crowd, and let the moment sink in. "From today, I declare the *sovereign* nation of Guayandes will no longer sell its oil to the imperialist devil. The *sovereign* nation of Guayandes will no longer import any tainted products from the foul imperialists in the north. The *sovereign* nation of Guayandes will reject any foreign aid from the dirty pig capitalists. Guayandes does not need them and their sanctimonious lectures, their tainted money wrapped in condescension. Guayandes needs only one thing: *sovereignty!*" The crowd erupted in joy.

***

President Evorez strutted back into the tent, elated. "Do you hear the crowds?" he asked his advisers and the top officials of Guayandes Petroleum, who had arranged the campaign show for him.

"It was an impressive demonstration, *Señor Presidente*, and we deeply appreciate your traveling to the jungle to see our work for yourself," said Javier Jimenez, the head of Guayandes Petroleum. "If I may, sir, while I have you here . . ." He looked anxious. He glanced at his staff and at the president's top adviser, Segundo Espina. "It's about the subsidies provided to the citizens of Guayandes."

"That is what sovereignty is all about!" said Evorez. "*Our* resources! *Our* money!"

"Sir, the thing is . . ." Jimenez wrung his hands. "We've been looking at some numbers. You see, Your Excellency, it costs Guayandes Petroleum twenty-eight times more money to get petroleum out of the ground than Guayandan consumers pay for it at the pump."

"I love hearing that! That is what *La Revolución* is all about! A *social* economy that favors *the people.*"

"The drawback, *Señor Presidente*, is that we are getting very little return. Guayandes Petroleum has no money."

"We are giving subsidies to the people. We can also give subsidies to Guayandes Petroleum."

"If I may, sir," Jimenez said cautiously. "If we no longer export oil to the United States, and we no longer accept foreign aid from them, where will we get money?"

"We will print more money," Evorez said, grabbing a donut from a table. "That is sovereignty!"

"This will lead to rather high inflation of the chavi, I'm afraid." Jimenez looked very uncomfortable.

Evorez turned to him, angered. "Inflation is a conspiracy of capitalism! It is the result of speculation by the imperialists, trying to steal our resources! We will not fall for this."

"The currency issue is only one difficulty we face. There is also the issue of the shortage of oil, due to, um, recent personnel changes here at Guayandes Petroleum. You can see the challenges."

Evorez looked taken aback. He pointed outside the tent. "I just discovered more oil for you!"

"Sir, we set up the survey equipment and the rig where we already knew there was oil and let you look through the lens and declare you found it. If we don't start exporting this oil, Guayandes will not have any hard currency left to invest in maintenance, to allow for the next discovery."

"Jimenez, as I am sure you are aware, I am running a campaign for reelection. Surely you understand the importance for me, and for this country, that rural voters maintain their access to subsidized petroleum. I trust you don't want me to lose their confidence and, thus, their vote."

"Of course not, Your Excellency. Your stewardship of Guayandes is most enlightened. Although—again, due to recent personnel changes—we are having difficulties meeting domestic demand for consumption, as well. There are very long lines at the gas stations."

"Those lines have been created by my opponents! They are a conspiracy to turn the people against me! They hire people to stand in line so that people like you will increase the price and gouge the Guayandan people, stealing from them *their very own resources!* You are stomping on *their sovereignty!*" He pounded a fist on the table in the middle of the tent. He turned to Segundo and pointed to Jimenez. "Fire him."

Segundo looked at Jimenez. Jimenez opened his mouth to speak. Segundo shook his head, his lips pursed. He looked at one of his security guards, who escorted Jimenez out.

CHAPTER SEVENTEEN

Ellie and Vanessa could hear Eminem blaring from the speakers as they walked up to the Marine House, where nearly the entire embassy staff, it seemed, were well on their way to drinking away a Friday evening. Oliver and the other kids ran off in different directions. Ellie went inside to get a drink. Out on the patio, three Marines in T-shirts and shorts juggled beers and barbecue tools as they manned two grills. American and Guayandan staff mingled and ate and drank, while slowly, collectively, they all got drunk.

Vanessa spotted Victor, who was standing with Wes, Simon, and Adam, all of whom were staring at Patrón. She walked over to them.

"The sheikh's niece grabbed my clothes off the floor of the gondola and left me there, naked. Thank god I still had my ushanka." Patrón turned to Vanessa. "We're swapping war stories. Join us."

Vanessa took a sip of Victor's beer and stepped in toward the group.

"I got arrested on my last tour," Wes said.

"That's a good story," Patrón said.

"I pissed off one of the higher ups in the police. I got a little too close to his deputy, so he decided to send me a message. But, since I was close with his deputy, the deputy called to warn me they were on their way to arrest me. I'm sitting watching *Goodfellas* when this guy calls me and says, hey, you're about to be arrested."

"What did you do?" asked Vanessa. "You're happy and comfy at home and then you get a call like that."

"I thought, I better put on some pants."

"Fair," said Ness.

Vanessa recognized this, the instant community created among people from a world so few knew or understood. They weren't allowed to share many of their experiences with most people in their lives, and even if they could, most people simply wouldn't get it. As a result, sharing with each other became a catharsis.

Who else could understand the nightmare of taking a polygraph exam, except someone who had been strapped to a box and swirled for hours while a weenie who had never left Virginia questioned that person about foreign contacts after he revealed his baker was Lebanese? Who else could appreciate the story about meeting an asset behind a pizzeria in the middle of a desert and sharing a camel's milk pizza on barely leavened crust while several goats roamed around? These weren't experiences they could share, even with good friends. Aside from the not-so-minor issue of such experiences being classified, only someone who had gone through similar absurdity could possibly understand the stress, the fear, or the rush.

Vanessa recognized the camaraderie such absurdity forged. People who perhaps would have nothing in common in the regular world could create the strongest of bonds due to their shared and rarefied experiences. She understood the need to talk about those experiences and the need to feel part of a community that understood them. She had felt the same camaraderie among her FBI buddies.

"I might need a drink to keep up with your war stories," she said.

"Great idea!" said Patrón. "I need a refill. Come on." He offered her his elbow. She hooked her arm through his and he led her inside the Marine House and to the bar, where two more buzz cuts were mixing drinks. One was chewing on a blue crayon. A group was shooting pool in a side room. Oliver and some of the other kids had started a foosball game. "What are you drinking?"

"Red wine, please," Ness said to the Marine with the crayon in his mouth.

"I'll have a gin and tonic, in two separate glasses," said Patrón.

"Two gin and tonics?" the Marine asked.

"No. Gin and tonic, in two separate glasses. One glass with gin. One with tonic."

Vanessa smiled. Patrón turned to her. "I'm a little worried you're going to get bored here, Vanessa. Why don't you come work for me?"

"In the same office with my husband? No, thank you."

"We like you more," he said.

"I'm sure that's true, but I'll pass. I'll work it out."

The Marine handed her a glass of wine and placed a glass of gin and a glass of tonic on the bar in front of Patrón. He took the glass of gin and turned away from the bar, leaving the glass of tonic sitting there, untouched.

"Ai, Papi!" a woman from the dance floor yelled at Patrón.

"You let me know if you change your mind," he said. "I don't have a position for you. Or a budget to pay you. But I bet Andy could figure it out." He turned to the woman who was undulating to the music. He hollered at her and shook his hips, his arms in the air—still holding his gin—as he made his way to her. Ness laughed and went outside to Victor, who was watching the debauchery slowly build across the entire community. Patrón's dance partner started twerking.

"She knows she's going to see all these people again on Monday, right?" asked Vanessa.

"I've never really deciphered it," Victor said. "I think people see a tour overseas as a chance to reinvent themselves, to leave behind whoever they were in Northern Virginia and let go of their inhibitions. It's probably healthy."

The woman on the dance floor turned her back to Patrón, pulled her skirt up to reveal a thong, and began rubbing her ass against him.

"Albeit, slightly unhygienic," Victor said.

"It's like a baboon," Vanessa said, unable to turn away from the spectacle. "The Lunch Bunch life coach would have a heyday psychoanalyzing this behavior."

"Ah, yes. How was it?"

"She told me transitions can be hard but if I stay positive, great things will happen."

"Sounds reasonable."

"Sounds like a fortune cookie."

Mike swaggered up to them, holding a beer. "Pretty tame party after Baghdad. Man, Baghdad officers know how to par-tay." He attempted to do some kind of a dance waving his hands over his head while he sang, "Woot woot! I'm telling you, every night was a beer fest. *Every fucking night!*"

"Every night?" Victor asked.

Mike seemed to realize this didn't make him look too serious about his mission in Iraq. "Nah, man. I'm exaggerating. Like, just most nights. Some nights. The other guys. I was too busy."

"How's your cultivated crop recruitment coming along?"

"I got three reports out today. Four more to finish Monday before my next meeting. Director's going to love it."

"You're doing your nation a great service," Victor said.

"I am," said Mike. "I think I'll get another beer to reward myself."

"You do that. You deserve it."

"What the fuck was that?" asked Vanessa, watching Mike head inside.

Mike passed through the crowd hovering between the grills and the bar and said, "Who deserves a beer? This guy." He pointed to himself, smiling and scanning the group for acknowledgment. They ignored him.

"Patrón is keeping him busy chasing low-hanging fruit. He produces lots of reports, which makes us look really busy as a station, and keeps Director off our back, while the rest of us work to take down the FRPT before they can completely take over Guayandes. Speaking of which, I'm going back to the jungle next week. I've got to meet my guy, calm him down. He must be freaking out from the Blackhouse stories."

"You go save the world. I'll be here. Ironing."

"We have a housekeeper for that."

"Shit."

"You'll figure it out." He pointed to the woman on the dance floor. "It's a chance to reinvent yourself!"

CHAPTER EIGHTEEN

Adam sat in the university atrium, sipping a coffee. Valentina was late.

He watched the students filing to and from class. They wore blue jeans, Nike sneakers, and Gap T-shirts. They drank Coca-Cola and carried Marvel comic books, while discussing the latest films out of Hollywood. Despite Evorez's constant indoctrination to try to get these young people to hate the United States, American soft power seemed to be prevailing. How would this generation respond as the consequences of Evorez's recent ban on imports from the United States started to manifest themselves?

Adam saw Valentina come into the atrium. She looked shook up but smiled as she crossed to where he was sitting.

"I'm sorry I'm late," she said. "I got robbed. Shall we go sit in the cafeteria?" She turned toward the glassed-in café.

"Wait, what?" Adam said, following her. "What happened? Are you OK?"

"It's fine. We're all fine. Do you want some more coffee?"

"What happened?"

She stopped in the middle of the atrium and looked at Adam. "A group in masks came into the apartment at dawn. They tied me and my parents up and held us at gunpoint. They took many things, but they are just things. We are fine. More often these days, this kind of robbery does not end up fine. Let's go get coffee."

They went into the cafeteria. Adam bought Valentina a coffee and joined her at their regular table.

"You're handling this really well," Adam said.

"They took nearly all our chavis. The problem is, inflation is so high now, the currency is almost worthless. We had piles and piles of chavis in the house. It took them several trips with suitcases to move all the chavis out. It was ridiculous. It ended better for us than for most. We were tied up and held at gunpoint. Many others end up in a ditch."

"Did they take everything?"

"Chavis? Yes. But they didn't find the currency that matters." She smiled. "Are you aware of the black market in Guayandes, Adam? Do you follow that at your American embassy? Your dollars are trading for chavis at sixty times the official rate. That will only go up as Guayandan inflation goes up. Have you seen the lines at the shops? People can't get the products they need. Instead of making it easier to import goods, Evorez fines the shopkeepers for creating long lines and making it hard for people to access products that simply don't exist. The hospitals are facing supply shortages, too."

"Surely, the Guayandan people see this is all a result of Evorez's economic policies?" Adam asked.

"The people don't understand. They only understand they are hungry and their children are hungry or their mother has died because the hospital couldn't help. Evorez blames it on the United

States. Capitalism brings speculation, which brings economic hardship. That in turn brings crime and corruption. The people then demand discipline and order. The police demonstrated. Evorez called it a coup. When a judge started to investigate it, he was replaced and asked to go into early retirement. Then Evorez fired the chief of police and announced a crackdown. The people only hear the message he yells over and over and over, that he is the only one who can bring discipline and order and safety. They do not understand the economic and political subtleties that got us here to begin with. Do you understand everything I just explained?" Valentina asked.

Adam nodded.

"Good. That means your Spanish has really improved."

CHAPTER NINETEEN

Victor sat at the long wooden bar in his Kiltoa hotel, waiting for Frank and Wes. The tarantula had moved to a corner near the television. Victor had suggested to Patrón that Mike stay in Guayita. Mike was deeply enmeshed in his research on crop production, and Director was enthusiastic about the number of reports coming from station. Patrón had agreed. Mike was visibly relieved.

Having someone with Frank's experience and Wes's ability provided some comfort before what was sure to be a complex meeting. Now that Lawrence Blackhouse had told the world the United States intelligence community was using Kapokom to listen in on FRPT leaders—and Victor knew that he and his colleagues, specifically, were the ones doing this—the stakes of the meeting were high and the risks of danger were real. Everyone was better off with Mike back in the capital poring over crop reports.

Frank came down the stairs and into the lobby, accompanied by one of the Marias. He was fully dressed. She was not. He dropped her at the couch with the other Marias and went to the bar. Wes arrived soon after. He looked at Victor's brown leather vest. "Have you ever watched Swedish porn, Victor?"

"I can't say I'm familiar with that particular subgenre of film, Wes."

"That vest belongs in Swedish porn movies."

"That's very helpful, particularly right before we head out into FRPT territory where we could die at any moment."

"You're welcome," Wes said.

The three discussed the plan one last time then went their separate ways.

To break up his walk to the meeting site, Victor stopped in a bodega to buy cigarettes.

"I'll take that pack there," Victor said, pointing.

"That's my last pack," the cashier said.

Victor pulled out a hundred and fifty chavis and placed them on the counter.

"I said that's my last pack. If I sell them to you, I won't have any left."

"That's true," Victor said.

"Then what do I tell the next guy who comes in asking to buy cigarettes?"

"That you don't have any."

"He would never shop here again. Why would someone shop at a store that doesn't sell them what they want?"

Victor slipped his money back in his pocket and wished the man a good day.

He walked farther out of the main part of town and crossed the plaza to a different alley where he'd have about two minutes to talk to El Gordo. With a glance, he saw both Wes and Frank in their designated positions. He relaxed a little, but only a little.

El Gordo was waiting behind a pile of broken wood, hiding in the darkening shadows. He was edgy. Victor could see him twitching, his head darting back and forth with every dog bark or tricycle squeak emanating from the town.

"Did you know about Kapokom?" he demanded. "Did you know Kapokom was compromised? Who is Blackhouse? What else does he know?"

Victor tried to calm him. Anxiety didn't produce good results. "Slow down. What did you hear about Kapokom?"

"The reports that the US was listening to us through Kapokom. Reis is trying to figure out who snitched to the Americans."

Victor understood his panic. El Gordo had not, in fact, been the one to inform the Americans that Reis, the leader of the FRPT, and his inner circle relied on Kapokom, but if a hunt was on for a snitch, that detail would hardly matter.

"Your government can't protect your secrets. How are you going to protect me?" he asked.

It was a fair question.

"Am I next? Is my name the next one to come out?"

"Stay focused, and stay calm. Look at me," Victor said. *"Look at me."* He leaned close to El Gordo, staring directly into his eyes. "I will not let you down. You have my word."

El Gordo blinked and breathed. He shook his head, resigned. He knew he trusted Victor. He knew he'd keep giving information. "They're moving off Kapokom after those reports. Reis is limiting cell phone use. They're switching to couriers whenever possible."

Victor assessed what El Gordo said. The good news was that FRPT operations would be severely slowed down if they had to rely on couriers to communicate. The bad news was that an incredibly rich intelligence stream—the full cell phone communications of FRPT leadership—had dried up, just like that, because some wanker had stolen intelligence and leaked it, claiming he supported transparency when, in fact, Victor and his team had simply been doing their job: spying on bad guys. Keeping El Gordo talking was that much more important now. Without the intelligence coming in directly from the group's communications, El Gordo was the best source they had.

"Evorez needs money for his election. The opposition is clamoring for his head after he fired everyone from Guayandes Petroleum. He's planning to ramp up his campaigning around the country. Reis is helping him. The FRPT needs Evorez to stay in office. Reis's position is dependent on Evorez's position."

"What kind of help exactly?"

"A large chunk of the cocaine profit is being funneled to Evorez's presidential campaign. FRPT soldiers are also painting El Toro symbols all over the north."

"Go back to that first thing you said."

"The FRPT is funneling cocaine money to the president of Guayandes."

Victor couldn't see Frank and Wes, but he could feel them getting agitated. It was time to wrap up the meeting and move out. "Go back. Stay calm. Get me anything you can on how the group is communicating now that Kapokom is out. And as many details about the relationship between Reis and Evorez as possible."

"I don't know if I can do it. They're looking for someone to blame, and they wouldn't be too far off target if they decided to blame me."

"I know you're scared, El Gordo. But I need you to trust me. Trust that I can keep you safe. Your safety is more important to me than any information you give me. If you need out, you tell me. But if you want to see Reis and the others go down, I need you to stick with me."

They reviewed the plan for their next meeting and Victor slipped El Gordo his payment plus a bonus, to help convince him to stick with Uncle Sam, despite Uncle Sam's inability to keep a secret. They disappeared into opposite alleyways and walked away.

CHAPTER TWENTY

Victor flung open the door to his apartment, his bag slung across his chest, his T-shirt emanating a malodorous combination of jungle dankness, recycled car air, and his own sweat. From the entrance, he could see Vanessa downstairs in the living room of the duplex, sitting on the pastel couch and staring out the two-story windows at the volcanoes in the distance. He dropped his bag and headed down the stairs. She continued staring outside.

"Jesus doesn't love me," she said as he approached her.

That's it, Victor thought. *My wife has cracked. She's found religion.*

"He was up there," she said, pointing up toward the top of the windows. "The light was so nice. He smiled at me, which was great, because we had never really had a relationship before."

"Maybe Lunch Bunch with that life coach wasn't a great idea," Victor said.

"Then he fell. He just fell. Right here. Almost broke his ankle."

"Jesus broke his ankle?"

"Didn't you see him by the garage, limping?"

He sat next to her. She became very animated all of a sudden. "What the fuck is that smell?" She turned to him. "Is that you?"

"Stop. Explain."

"Jesus, the guy who does maintenance for the apartment building, came to help me clean the windows. I hadn't wanted to ask him; he always seems annoyed by me. But I did, and he said yes, and he came with this giant ladder and climbed up and started cleaning and then *boom!* Fell right off the ladder. He left all pissy, like it was my fault. You see? Jesus doesn't love me."

Victor was laughing now. "*Hay-soos*. Not Jesus. You scared me for a minute."

"I know it's pronounced *Hay-soos*. But you and I speak English together. When I say the word Mexico to you, I don't say *Meh-hee-koh*. I say Mexico."

"So you didn't have the time of your life while I was in the jungle?"

"Where shall I start? The school called to tell me I was the only mother who hadn't volunteered to help make posters for Future Global Leaders Day. They wanted my help scanning in photos of all the children to morph with faces of historic leaders and photoshop them onto their bodies. Like morphing Oliver's face with Charles de Gaulle's and then pasting it onto de Gaulle's uniformed body."

"Oliver won't be as tall as de Gaulle. Maybe Nelson Mandela?"

Vanessa looked at him and blinked. "I think you're missing the more important points here. Then Oliver came home with his spelling list and one of the words was f-l-e-m."

"Phlegm?"

"Yes, but spelled f-l-e-m. I wrote the teacher a note and told her it was incorrect. Oliver comes home with a second spelling list and a note from the teacher, apologizing for the mistake and explaining the word is spelled f-l-e-g-m."

"Flegm?"

"Future global leaders, my ass! I send another note, telling her it's still spelled incorrectly. This time, she just took it off the spelling list. Why does a first grader need to know what phlegm is, let alone how to spell it?"

Victor reached for Vanessa's hands but couldn't grasp them, as she kept talking animatedly. She was on a roll.

"Then the internet goes out. So the guy had to come. At the same time, I got the final bill for our internet back in Washington, and it's wrong. I'm dealing with getting new internet here, while also trying to close out our internet there. And these women! It's like fucking Real Housewives, US Embassy edition. I invited Ellie to lunch. Then I got a call from Savannah wondering why Ellie and I had gone to lunch alone, instead of calling Savannah and Christie and Rebecca and Abby to join us. It's like a twisted reality TV show. Throw together a bunch of overeducated spouses of bureaucrats with incredibly strong opinions who would never hang out with each other in real life, place them in a bizarre location that tests their cultural, gastronomical, and political sensitivities, and watch them interact with each other and with the locals. In fact, I'm going to pitch that idea to some Hollywood producer. I'm sure it would sell." She stood up now, agitated. "Then, I ran into Patrón at the embassy when I went to check the mail. Turns out, Savannah complained to him that Ellie and I are spending too much time together."

"What?"

"She told him she thinks it's not good for 'cover reasons' that we are seen together. That it's not good for anyone's security."

"What the fuck does she know about cover and security? What did Patrón say?"

"He didn't give a shit. She's just trying to break us up because we didn't invite her to lunch! Then, after he left, I ran into Christie, and *she* berates me for going to lunch without her. Then she asked *where* we went to lunch. I told her, and she starts to complain about the restaurant. She's complaining about the fucking restaurant she wasn't invited to! Then she starts yapping about how bad restaurants are here and how much she doesn't like the place anyway and it will never compare to her time in Riyadh."

"Riyadh?"

"I know, right? She totally loved Riyadh because she lived in a compound with a Safeway. Like living in fucking Clarendon. Why the fuck do these people go overseas?" She was pacing frantically now. "Then I went to the grocery store and they were playing Air Supply. I kid you not. I haven't heard Air Supply since 1986, but at the grocery store, they were playing it on a loop. For *forty fucking minutes* I had to listen to *Lost in Love*. Look, it's catchy, don't get me wrong, but maybe it was a little too much this week. I bet they don't play Air Supply in Riyadh." Vanessa stopped pacing and turned to Victor, wild eyed. "What is happening to me?"

Victor pulled her down to the couch. "Relax. I've seen this before. I call it Dependent Syndrome."

"What the fuck is Dependent Syndrome?"

"Take a very successful and ambitious person and make him or her a dependent of a government bureaucrat overseas, with few satisfying professional options, and watch the implosion as the community heaps mounds of insignificant bullshit on them. It's quite something."

"Am I going to survive it?"

"You're going to more than survive it. You're going to overcome it and thrive. I just know it." He put his arms around her and pulled her head to his chest.

"Victor," she said.

"Yes, love."

"I love you and you're a great husband. But please go shower."

"Yes, dear."

CHAPTER TWENTY-ONE

Victor passed through the heavy bulletproof glass doors into the main chancery. Light was streaming in through the atrium and a few employees from various offices were settled into different nooks, strategizing, problem solving, or, more likely, gossiping. He went into the cafeteria and bought a coffee. Ellie was behind a counter, stacking boxes.

"What are you doing, Ellie?"

"Helping with cafeteria inventory. They asked for volunteers, so here I am!" She yelled over her shoulder, "Hey, Jorge! Do you want these here or over on the other side?"

Victor came back out into the sunny open space and saw Laura at one of the tables. As the Guayandan Foreign Ministry had ordered, Ambassador Jones had left Guayandes a few days earlier. It would take the White House a long time to nominate a new ambassador. It hardly mattered. Congress was so caught up in a budget fight, the Senate would never get around to confirming the person anyway. Laura remained in charge of the embassy. Her eyes were glazed over and she looked forlorn. He sat down across from her. "Another casualty of the life of the embassy community? Or a boss beaten down by the bureaucracy?"

"Number two," she said with a smile. "Ask me about number one after the next happy hour at the Marine House."

"Red tape strikes again. Tell me."

"More like red tape strangling me slowly. So very, very slowly. The airplane with Ambassador Jones has barely left Guayandan air space, and I have to give President Evorez fifty million dollars. Worse, he doesn't want it. He and Segundo were on TV this morning calling it *capitalismo cerdo*."

"To be fair, we *are* capitalist pigs," Victor said. "Why are we giving them fifty million dollars they don't want?"

"Congress was a little too *pro forma*. Every year, they sign off on a set amount of foreign aid to a list of countries. Guayandes is on the list. After Jones was kicked out last week, I told Valencia to make sure Guayandes was taken off the list."

"He didn't."

She shook her head. "One congressional staffer crossing out Guayandes. That's all I needed. Now I have fifty million dollars I have to give to a country that just booted our ambassador and has publicly stated doesn't want the money."

"Can Congress take the money back?"

"I asked. It's never been done. The bureaucracy doesn't know how to do it."

"Countries tend to want our money, even if they complain about us."

"Evorez is ready to put his money where his mouth is. Or not put money there, I guess."

"You'll convince him. Even diehard socialists tend to come around when they smell the cash."

"Evorez barks loudly. Normally, I'd meet with some counter-parts at the Ministry of Foreign Affairs or some well-respected members of the business community to take the temperature, feel out people's reactions to developments, but nobody will meet with me. The Blackhouse document dump included several cables I wrote to Washington. I listed people by name, Victor. Now it's all over the news they were meeting with me. I can't get a single one to answer the phone. The fact that I called Evorez a buffoon in one cable also didn't help."

"Are they going to kick you out, too?"

"With this government, anything is possible."

He left Laura and headed to the Men's Locker Room. He punched in his code and went through the doors, through the cubicle farm, and to his desk. Andy was hunched over Victor's computer, staring intensely at the screen.

"Hey, Andy. Uh, what's up?"

Andy jumped. He looked up at Victor. "Hey, man!" He took a swig of a Red Bull sitting on Victor's desk. "You were due for some computer security training. 'Work Station Securitization.' It's an online course. It rhymes. Takes about thirty minutes. Director said you were due to take it and couldn't log on until it was done. So Patrón asked me to do it for you. I just finished Wes's course. I'll do Simon's next. I'll be out of your way in a minute." His eyes were bloodshot and he had run his hand through his hair so many times that it stood up straight. It was a Robert Downey Jr. in *Less Than Zero* look. Victor had to admit, Andy kind of scared him. Victor didn't say a word and backed out of his own office slowly. Andy downed the rest of the Red Bull and went back to clicking through a Power Point presentation.

Safely out in the main part of the Men's Locker Room, Victor turned toward Patrón's office and bumped into Mike, who was carrying stacks of papers covered in colored graphs.

"How's the food security recruitment coming along, Mike?" He tilted his head as he read the title on the top page of the stack. *"Equatorial Crop Rotation and Long-Term Implications of Soil Tillage on Southwest Facing Slopes.* That seems rather specific."

"It is, Victor. It is. The analyst at Director *loves* it! This guy isn't even officially recruited yet, and he's handing me documents. Maize. Cacao. Soybeans. The list goes on. I want to go slowly, though. We really need this recruitment. I don't want to spook him."

"Sounds like you're on the right track. You just keep luring him in slowly. You'll hook him."

Mike smiled and nodded his head a little. Victor could almost hear Mike telling himself, "Yes, I can do this. I am the man who can do this." Mike walked to his office with the pep that comes with renewed confidence. He was going to bag the corn man.

Victor circled around some cubicle dividers and popped his head into Patrón's office. Adam sat across from the chief, riveted.

"That's the last time I'll ever use a kitten operationally, that's for sure." Patrón sat back in his chair and took a sip of coffee. For a moment, he looked lost in reverie. Adam looked like he couldn't breathe. A caiman alligator that had been stuffed and mounted watched them both from his perch in the corner.

"Chief?" Victor said carefully. Patrón and Adam both turned to him, each shaking off his haze.

"Come in, Victor. Have a seat." He looked at Adam. "Go get hunting, Adam. Or you'll have to recruit one of Mike's crop developmentals. What do you know about sorghum?" The word made Adam anxious and he darted out of the room. "I'm glad you stopped by. I've got something I need to talk to you about."

Victor sat where Adam had been. The caiman eyed him.

"Do you follow Washington at all, Victor?"

"Not if I can avoid it."

"Smart man. It seems we may be heading toward a government shutdown." Patrón pulled a flask out of a desk drawer and poured a little clear liquid into his coffee. "The weasels in Congress are in a nip-twisting fight over the budget. Instead of hammering it out, they plan to inconvenience everybody."

"I was in DC during a shutdown once. I was considered a nonessential employee. I had nearly two weeks off. I ate a lot of ice cream. It was actually rather convenient."

"Good to see you can be flexible for your government in demanding times."

"I do what I can. I just saw Laura. Evorez doesn't want the fifty million dollars she's trying to give him. Fifty million would keep us running for, what, a few hours or so, right?"

"I know, we have to give money to a guy who doesn't want it, while we shut down operations for lack of funds. We'd both be surprised, except we aren't. In any case, I'm not sure yet if or how a shutdown would affect us. I consider us all essential employees, so we'd keep working no matter what. Except maybe Mike."

"We're catching bad guys and stamping out drug trafficking," Victor said. "Seems like an easy case to make. Food crop security might be a harder sell."

"The analyst is loving those reports, and she's writing tons of her own reports from them. We're generating a lot of electronic paper. Director loves it. All the appearances of hard, consequential work with none of the actual consequences. While nobody is looking, you keep focusing on the bad guys and the drugs." He began stroking the caiman. "Did you read the Director cable about the Blackhouse leaks?" Patrón looked up at Victor. "I didn't either. Andy got the rundown from Sergio and told me. He's going to turn into a bull's testicle with all that caffeine shit flowing through his veins." Patrón poured a little more tequila into his coffee cup. "Go see Sergio, and see if you can pry that bull dick serum away from Andy before he explodes."

Victor walked past his office. Andy was staring at the screen, his eyes bloodshot. He was clicking through the security quiz at high speed and summarizing the rules out loud. "Don't click the link, motherfucker. Dipshit password D-I-P-S-H-I-T. Don't share your password, even if Svetlana swears she loves you."

From across the cubicles, Mike screamed. Adam, Wes, and Simon popped up. Victor walked toward Mike's office.

"It's not mine, I swear to god. I have no idea how this got here. I would never, Victor. Never."

Victor looked down at the open filing cabinet drawer in Mike's office. Nestled in the corner was a plastic bag wrapped in duct tape. It was full of white powder. Victor looked out across the cubicle farm. Wes smirked and disappeared back into his cubicle.

"I'm disappointed, Mike," Victor said.

Patrón came to Mike's office door. He looked down at the bag and up at Mike's ashen face. He pulled out a switchblade. Mike grew paler. Patrón looked as though he were reaching for Mike, but leaned down instead to pick up the bag. He slit a small hole in the side and poured some of the white substance into his coffee cup. He took a sip. "Much better." He threw the bag at Mike. "Stop hoarding the sugar. Put it back by the coffee machine." He went back to his office.

Victor heard Wes laugh inside his cubicle. Mike exhaled.

"Very funny, guys. Make me look like a drug dealer. Hilarious."

Wes clicked on the speakers and turned up the Reggaeton. Mike closed his office door.

Victor went to the unmarked door on the fifth floor of the building. He pushed the buzzer in long and short bursts—*buzzzz, buzz buzz, buzzzz, buzz, buzzzz, buzz buzz buzz*—until it clicked open.

"You know one buzz is sufficient," Sergio said.

"I was doing the super secret buzz signal, so you'd know it was me."

"There's a camera at the door. I can see it's you."

"That's less fun," Victor said.

"Anyway, I knew you were coming because we implanted a listening device in your arm while you were sleeping so we can have access to your every thought."

"Sounds reasonable."

"But thanks to the Blackhouse leaks, my previously unlimited powers are now, sadly, limited. The new regulations are a little complicated, so let me deal with the lawyers. In a nutshell, we must file a report with the lawyers to collect signals intelligence on anyone who has ever called the United States. We cannot collect on a Tuesday. When collecting on a foreign leader, if the leader is an ally at the time of collection, it is illegal to collect. If the leader is not an ally, we can collect. For example, if we were to discover that Saudi Arabia helped fund al-Qaeda, we could collect on them that day. But the next day, when they provide some intel on the location of a terrorist, even if they helped fund him, they are our ally and we cannot collect. It's very simple and makes perfect sense. As for collecting SIGINT on US citizens, don't."

"That's it?"

"Like I said, it's a little more complicated, but leave it to me to deal with the lawyers. In the meantime, we still have one program Blackhouse didn't leak, at least not yet." Sergio handed Victor a piece of paper.

"They have a fucking submarine?"

"Don't look at me, man. I just collect the conversations."

Victor walked slowly back to the Men's Locker Room. The FRPT was using a submarine to move drugs up the river without being detected. The group had to have more money than Victor and his crew realized. They were funding Evorez and felt free to dock a submarine in Guayandan territory? Tamindo's decapitation strikes weren't doing enough. The FRPT was becoming a giant corporation funding the president of Guayandes. The two main groups causing instability in Guayandes were working hand in hand.

Victor walked into the office and past the chart that showed FRPT leaders, some with red Xs across their photos. The organization was a true criminal enterprise backed up with sizeable assets. Cutting off the head, over and over, as the Tamindo military had been doing for years, wouldn't be enough to neutralize them.

Victor and his team needed a new approach.

CHAPTER TWENTY-TWO

Vanessa strapped Oliver into his seatbelt and drove out onto the well-maintained road surrounded by carefully curated landscaping. She glanced over at Paxico volcano, rising in the distance under a clear blue sky. Enormous green fronds waved on the breeze and bromeliads and heliconia flowers were bursting red and orange. It was beautiful.

She drove past the guardhouse, waving at the man she now always called Jorge, and out into the adjacent compound where Evorez's house was. A gate had been installed at the bottom of the road that led to the house. Six soldiers with very large guns stood outside the gate.

"That sure is welcoming, isn't it, Oliver?"

The new security measures didn't surprise her. Evidence of a massive crackdown had been showing up everywhere in the weeks since Evorez had implemented a state of emergency. A tank now stood guard at the main entrance to the residential compound where Evorez's private house was, and armed men and armored personnel carriers dotted the city. Police blockades popped up with regularity and car searches—and the bribes that went with them—were increasingly frequent. Although she refused to admit that these developments had affected her, Ness would occasionally allow that she had stopped going out in the city as often as before.

The light turned red. She considered whether to stop. Roadside robberies were also increasing. She idled at the light. "Let's play a game, Oliver," she said. "Look all around the car. If you see anyone coming up to us, you yell, 'Kabinga!'"

He giggled. She felt sad she needed to enlist her six-year-old son's help like this.

She drove past a group of stray dogs and a dirt pitch where young Guayandans were playing a game of soccer, a dirt cloud puffing up around them. A man who was hunched over pushed an open wooden cart full of car parts. She passed a small tin house where a young girl was selling corn on the cob that her mother was grilling behind it. Ness turned the corner into Ellie's compound. A guard waved her through that gatehouse and she found herself in another quiet residential compound. She made her way to the playground and parked just as her phone pinged.

Ness looked at the text from Ellie.

> Sorry, late! Helping Jorge sort mail at the embassy. Be there soon.

"Heidi and her mom will be here in a few minutes," Ness said, as she helped Oliver jump down from the car. He ran to the swings, where a woman was pushing a little girl in dark braids. The woman was elegantly dressed in a fashionable silk blouse and leggings and very high-heeled suede boots that were common for wealthy mothers at walled-in Guayandan playgrounds, but Vanessa wondered how she didn't sink into the ground. The woman looked familiar.

"Miss Natalia's class," Vanessa said.

"We met at back to school night," the woman said. "I'm Claudette. How did your one hundred sixty cupcakes with vegan frosting turn out?"

Vanessa laughed. "I brought a five-pound bag of sugar to class instead and told the kids to open their mouths for a free for all."

"That's much more to their liking, I'm sure."

Cristiana and Oliver jumped off the swings in unison and ran to the playground's mini zip line. Claudette and Vanessa went to a picnic table and continued chatting. Vanessa found Claudette charming and interesting. She was clearly an intellectual, but seemed to have allowed herself—or forced herself—to morph into the more traditional role of women in Guayandes, running the household and keeping everything smooth for her husband. Vanessa sensed some of the rebel remained. Claudette talked a good talk, but she wasn't fully comfortable in her role.

Vanessa's phone pinged; another message from Ellie.

Jorge's got a package for you. Want me to take it for you?

She was like the mayor of the embassy, Vanessa thought. She responded.

Yes, please. But soon. When sun goes down, I go home.

With the recent uptick in crime, Vanessa and Victor had decided Oliver needed to be home, behind locked doors, by sunset. Life was idyllic behind walls.

Claudette stood up. "We must go now, but it was a pleasure to see you. I'm sure we'll see each other around, maybe at the next parent coffee at the school."

"Absolutely, or, you know, maybe just around," Vanessa stammered, knowing she'd never be at a parent coffee. Claudette lifted Cristiana and her braids into the car and drove away. Ness waved after her, as Ellie parked and waved back at Vanessa.

***

Sitting on the porch drinking wine that evening, Victor and Ness followed the time-honored tradition of married couples everywhere and debriefed each other on their day. Ness laughed at the image of Andy, high on Red Bull, taking every officer's online security training for them, zipping through the slides and clicking through the quiz questions. "Adam wanted to do the training himself," Victor said. "He's too good a kid. I diverted his attention with a river submarine loaded with drugs."

"Excuse me?"

Victor explained as much as he could about the submarine. Some amount of sharing among husband and wife was expected and even necessary in this clandestine world, but certain lines could never be crossed, and not only for the safety of the operation. Knowing intelligence was a real burden, Ness understood. If she didn't know the information in the first place, no one could get it from her under duress. When dealing with terrorists and drug traffickers and the like, that was safer.

"How was your day?" he asked, pouring her more wine.

"No cocaine on submarines, but I met a nice woman. We had met briefly at the school a while back, but chatted at the park today. She's quite knowledgeable about Guayandes. Her husband is from here and she's lived here for seven years now. I mentioned that Guayandan restaurant downtown I heard about at Lunch Bunch. She said Segundo's sister runs it and it's really good."

"Who is Segundo?"

"Claudette's husband."

"Who is Claudette?"

"The nice woman I met at the playground. Her daughter is in Oliver's class."

"Wait," Victor said. "What's their last name?"

"We didn't get that far. It was more kids and restaurants than family details and foreign contacts," Ness said. "I see where you're going with this. Can I have a friend without her being a target?"

"It depends who your friend is. Do you have a school directory?"

Vanessa grabbed it out of her desk and brought it to the porch. She flipped it open to Oliver's class and glanced through the names. "Cristiana, here." She pointed.

"Espina." Victor looked at Vanessa. "Segundo Espina is President Evorez's number two."

"Is that why he's called Segundo?" she asked.

"No, that's his name."

"Is he the second born in his family?"

"Fifth. But he's Evorez's closest adviser. Which means . . ." He gave Vanessa a charming smile.

"No. That's not what this means."

"Claudette is your new best friend."

"Her daughter is in Oliver's class, for fuck's sake."

"That gives you plenty of opportunity to spend time with her."

Vanessa sighed. "Using our kid?"

"Do you want him to grow up in a world where narco-traffickers run wild and free? Or do you want to once again work in the service of your country to help make the world a safer place for the next generation of Americans?"

"Cue the patriotic music. I'm waiting for a giant American flag to unfurl behind you."

"Come on! You're going to love it! You'll be back doing the job you love."

"I'm not getting paid for this."

"You get the satisfaction of knowing that a grateful nation thanks you," Victor said.

"Can I buy stilettos with that gratefulness? Anyway, the nation won't know about it."

"Once this is all declassified, in twenty-five—"

"Fifty."

"Fifty years, you can sell your story for millions."

"I'll be too old for stilettos at that point. She wants me to go to a parent coffee next week."

"Then you go to the parent coffee next week."

"I don't like coffee. Or parents."

Victor topped off their glasses. "You're going to love this. We're going to have so much fun." He clinked his glass against hers and drank. She knew he was right but suppressed a smile. Then she drank, too.

CHAPTER TWENTY-THREE

President Evorez slumped down in the driver's seat of the taxi and rubbed his backside on the massage ball padding that lined the seat. He sniffed the air and turned to his assistant, who hung a coconut air freshener from the rearview mirror. The taxi was parked in the driveway of his private home. Evorez rolled down his window and waved at the camera, which captured the brightly decorated, ceramic wall-slash-fountain surrounded by flowers that decorated his thick front lawn. The cameraman slid into the back seat. Evorez turned to the camera. "*¡Vámonos!*"

The president had had a difficult few weeks. Saying he was blocking imports from the imperialist swine had made for good television, but the real world consequences were proving economically inconvenient. With no new fishing nets, Guayandan fishermen were spending more time repairing nets than actually fishing, leading to a much smaller haul. Meanwhile, Guayandes Petroleum, the juggernaut of the economy, was ailing. The number of on-the-job accidents had increased tenfold since Evorez had fired the more experienced workers, and refining capacity had dwindled. He had long provided his people with cheap gasoline; he couldn't take that away now, it would cost him votes. But with less output, and so much of it marked for domestic consumption, Guayandes Petroleum had very little oil left to export. Guayandes was short on official cash.

That hadn't affected Evorez and those immediately around him. He allowed his ministers and aides to take care of their families. They were the first line of defense for the revolution, after all. But now the people, ordinary people, were beginning to agitate. The shopkeepers found it hard to stock their shelves. With no access to cash or imports, how could they buy any goods to sell?

Evorez needed to reassert control, to remind his people that sometimes the revolution required sacrifice, but to reassure them they were not alone in the struggle. "The people need to see you up close," Segundo had said to him. "They need to see you are among them. That you care for them. That you are *one of them*."

Evorez drove the taxi onto the clean, paved road in front of his house, past three rows of security guards, and through a heavily fortified gate he had recently installed after his interior minister had warned him about an uptick in crime—"Counter-revolutionists, likely funded by the United States," he had assured the president. The president couldn't remember the last time he had driven through Guayita on his own.

Once out of his compound, he turned to the camera in the back seat. "Our beautiful capital, Guayita!" he said, making a sweeping motion with one hand. The car hit a pothole and Evorez bounced so high he hit his head on the ceiling. "*¡Mierda!*" He turned to face forward and grabbed the wheel with both hands to get the car under control. The cameraman fumbled with the camera, which he had nearly dropped. Evorez drove down Amazonas Avenue. "Our most famous avenue," he said to the rearview mirror. The cameraman filmed his reflection. "Che himself rode his motorcycle down this beautiful street, bringing stories of the revolution to the people!"

Hundreds of people were on the side of the road, waiting in line to get into the grocery store, one of the few that had recently received a shipment of goods. "Look at all the Guayandans that have come out to greet us today!" Evorez said to the camera. The camera panned outside for a panoramic view. A giant black bull was painted on a red background on a wall. Someone had written on top of the bull in bright yellow letters, "*¿Líder o ladrón?*" Leader or thief? The cameraman swiftly focused the lens back on Evorez.

The taxi pulled into a plaza in a small town outside the capital. Green, blue, and red balloons and streamers lined the square. Children ran around chasing each other, dogs nipping at their ankles in excitement. An older gentleman handed out bright pink-and-blue cotton candy puffs. A young woman pushed a red popcorn cart through the crowd. An energizing samba beat blasted from speakers around the plaza. Evorez stepped out of the taxi.

The people swarmed around him, cheering and chanting, "El Toro! El Toro! El Toro!" He grinned and shook hands and patted children on their heads, mussing their hair. He kissed a baby and raised her high above the crowd. He held out an apple, and with a sleight of hand made it disappear. The crowd gasped. Evorez leaned toward a young girl in pigtails and reached behind her ear, where there appeared a candy bar. The people delighted in the magic. The little girl's brother snatched the candy bar and ran away. She screamed after him.

Evorez approached another child, a curly-haired boy with big, brown eyes. The samba music continued to pulse over the square. The president reached into his pocket and whipped out a long balloon. He blew it up and twisted and turned it. The boy watched him in wonder. A moment later, Evorez held up the balloon, which he had molded into the shape of a pig. The boy grinned and jumped up and down, trying to grab the pig. Evorez placed his hand on the boy's head. "Calm, my boy. I am not finished." The president again reached into his pocket. He flourished a large pin and, as the little boy watched, Evorez pricked the pig balloon. *Pop!* It exploded, and sad pieces of broken rubber fluttered down into the boy's hair. He started wailing.

Evorez laughed and addressed the crowd. "Young boy, children, all of you! We will prick the American swine until they fall apart!" The crowd applauded. The boy continued crying. "We will continue to fight! Remember, we are not alone. We have allies! There are many who want to see the imperialists destroyed! To see them pay a price for their arrogance! That is why, today, I am announcing to you, to the world, that Guayandes is offering political asylum to Lawrence Blackhouse, who risked his life to share with the world the evils of the nefarious imperialist pigs. I invite him here, to live and to build a new life and to contribute to our revolution. To fight for transparency of those who aim to control us, of those whose objective is to take away our sovereignty. They will never take away our sovereignty!"

CHAPTER TWENTY-FOUR

Victor grabbed a coffee mug off his desk and looked inside. It was clean enough, he decided, and he crossed the cubicle farm to the coffee pot. Taylor Swift played softly on the overhead speakers. Victor saw Mike approaching from the other side of the office and made a show of pouring sugar from the duct-taped plastic bag into his coffee. "That'll get me going, right, Mike? A little kicker for my coffee? How's the crop rotation investigation going? Should I invest in Guayandan soybeans? And who the fuck put on Taylor Swift?"

"Cacao is where it's at, Victor. Forget soybeans. Cacao and avocados. But cacao, wow. It's a good year for cacao. A good year for Taylor Swift, too, by the way." He added vanilla creamer to his coffee. "The analyst at Director and I cross-referenced the last fifty years of weather data with current weather trends and technological advances in crop cultivation at specific altitudes and their respective geo-coordinates here in Guayandes. It's a little technical, but suffice it to say, cacao is going to be booming this year. Taylor Swift's going to have a good year, too."

Andy emerged from behind a closed door. Victor and Mike both turned. They hadn't known he was in the office. He was in the same clothes as the day before, a Clash T-shirt with the words "London Calling" half tucked into his skinny jeans. He was holding a Red Bull. "Morning, gentlemen," he said. He chugged what was left in the Red Bull can, reached into the refrigerator behind Mike, and cracked open another. His eyes were red.

"Breakfast of champions," Victor said to him. "Did you sleep here last night?"

"No."

"You're wearing the same clothes."

"I was here all night. But I didn't sleep. You're all getting promoted."

"What?" asked Victor.

"Everyone's performance evaluation is due this week."

"I had totally forgotten about that. I'll write something up. At some point," Victor said.

"I wrote it."

"Good for you. I'll try to get to mine soon."

"No. I wrote *your* evaluation," Andy said. "Patrón said you guys had a lot going on this week. He asked me to write them. You've done a stellar job achieving your objectives and contributing to the mission. I'm betting you'll get promoted. All of you will." Andy gave a small nod in Mike's direction—Mike was making jazz hands and shaking them as Taylor sang *Shake It Off*—and whispered to Victor, "Not him." Then he announced, "Taylor's done." He switched the music and Reggaeton came on at the exact moment Wes walked in and said loudly, "Fuck yes, Reggaeton!"

Victor looked at Andy. "How did you know he was about to come in?"

"I'm a support officer, Victor. I'm here to support my officers." He disappeared into his office.

Victor took his coffee to Wes's cubicle. "How was your night?"

Wes emptied his pockets, tossing his keys, his wallet, and a tactical folding knife onto his desk before sitting down. He picked up a baton, flicked it to expand it, and leaned back in his ergonomic chair, while tapping the baton on the palm of his hand. "I met up with VZCUCUMBER last night."

"Your airport source?"

"He said there's been an uptick in activity lately, with shipments coming from the north and being flown out."

Adam, Simon, and Sergio came in the Men's Locker Room. Patrón came out of his office. They all perched on the side of the cubicle so they could listen.

"Can he confirm what kind of shipments?" Victor asked.

"He's got access to the bills of lading. They list avocados. He can't physically inspect the produce."

"Maybe it's nothing nefarious. Mike said the avocado crop is good this year. Maybe they really are boxes of avocados."

"They're using terminal four and the cargo comes in under military escort."

"Terminal four?" Victor asked. "Is VZCUCUMBER sure?"

Wes nodded.

"Terminal four is reserved," Victor said.

"For the president and his family." Wes smacked the baton against his palm again.

Victor could think of no reason why Evorez would be flying avocados out of the country. The cargo was almost certainly something else. Was Evorez allowing the FRPT to use his personal airport terminal to fly cocaine out of Guayandes?

"Who is going in and out?" Victor asked.

"VZCUCUMBER got ahold of the passenger manifests. They're all members of Evorez's family. They go with diplomatic passports. Over the past week, one flight went to Miami and one to New York, each with a stopover in Curaçao." Wes pulled documents out of his backpack, detailing VZCUCUMBER's information, including a copy of a recent bill of lading, a flight path registration, and photocopies of the diplomatic passports of two of President Evorez's nephews, neither of whom held any official position within the government.

The guys looked at each other for a few seconds. Finally, Sergio said, "It's a fucking family business."

"My guess is Segundo is coordinating it," Victor said.

"I think you're right," Adam said. "Evorez doesn't do anything without Segundo's approval. Although Evorez doesn't recognize that. Segundo does a good job letting Evorez think he's in charge."

"They're all taking their share, that's for sure," Wes said. "But VZCUCUMBER is only one source. Before we go claiming the president of Guayandes is involved in international drug trafficking with a revolutionary Marxist group, it would be nice to have some corroboration."

They all looked at Sergio. "Sorry, guys. With the ECHO program shut down, we've got no technical collection on either FRPT leadership or presidential communications. You're going to have to go the old-fashioned route." He turned to Victor, who looked anxious.

Patrón spoke up. "I know the purpose of implementing the ECHO program on Kapokom was to limit your trips to the jungle."

"It's getting hairy out there. More and more FRPT are crossing over from Tamindo. Kiltoa is not a safe place."

"Without the Kapokom stream, VZSPARKLEPONY is our best source for FRPT intelligence. You're the right case officer for the job, Victor. You know human intelligence operations better than anyone in this office. We're going to have to take the risk. You'll have Frank and Wes with you."

Wes smacked the baton onto his palm again. He looked Victor in the eye. "I got your back, *amigo*."

"I appreciate that."

"But one thing I will not compromise on, my dude."

Victor waited.

"We play Reggaeton during the car ride."

Victor turned to Patrón. "I can't work under these conditions, chief. It's a hostile work environment."

"The FRPT is proving a formidable foe," Patrón said. "Suggestions?"

"We won't be able to take it apart with a military approach," said Adam. "Tamindo's military takes one guy out and another one takes his place. And with two avenues to get the drugs out, a fucking submarine and a presidential airplane—which means presidential security—I don't know how you dismantle the group."

"We have to make it as expensive as possible to operate," said Victor. "Disrupt them to the point it is no longer a financially viable business plan. We keep taking out their leadership, with top priority being Reis. At the same time, we take out their main avenues for making money: the plane and the submarine. How?"

"Sabotage," said Wes. They all looked at Simon.

Simon looked back at them with a quizzical look. "Why are you looking at me?"

"You're the tech guy," said Wes. "How do we fuck with them?"

"Blast Reggaeton into the jungle," said Victor.

"Why are you always hating on Reggaeton, Victor?" asked Wes.

"We could hack their main computers. Put in malware," said Simon. "Or sabotage the machinery they use to refine the drugs."

"We could sink their submarine," Adam said.

"Look at the new guy," said Sergio. "Going full Steven Seagal. I'm proud of you."

"We have to find it first," Wes said.

"Can't we find it with satellite imagery?" Adam asked.

"If you know where to look," said Simon. "We don't."

"It might be near Esperanza. Valentina said her dad flies Segundo up to that area sometimes."

"That seems too far from the river," said Patrón.

"We need to keep taking out their leadership so it's expensive to fill the top jobs, and hard to find anyone willing to take the position," said Victor.

The office doorbell rang. They looked at the monitor and saw Laura smiling and waving to the camera outside. Simon buzzed her in.

Patrón said, "Wes, write up your meeting with VZCUCUMBER. Adam and Simon, go study ship engineering, in case we get more on the submarine. Victor, you've got a trip to plan." Patrón looked at Sergio. "And you, go back to the fifth floor."

Sergio smiled at Patrón and Laura. "There is no fifth floor, boss." He left.

Laura sat down in Patrón's office. The stuffed caiman was wearing a sash that said, "Miss Guayandes."

"I managed to talk to someone over at the Ministry of Foreign Affairs finally," Laura said. "Evorez is serious about the Blackhouse asylum offer."

"I'm not surprised. Does Main State have anything to say about it?"

"Valencia wrote an official statement. It rhymes."

"He wrote him another poem?"

"He asked me to send over an Edible Arrangement. I'm procrastinating as long as I can. Maybe Congress will shut down the government before I have to choose between a bucket of melon confetti and pineapple chunks in the shape of a bull. Valencia would also like Guayita Station to stand down on operations."

"Duly noted, and duly ignored. It would be a real kick in our ass if Evorez accepted Blackhouse. Could you threaten to withhold the fifty million dollars?"

"Evorez has said publicly he doesn't want it."

"Socialists tend to say that, until they think they might not actually get the cash."

"In any case, the money is mandated by Congress. Even if the government shuts down, the money is already allocated and has to be given."

"Evorez doesn't know that."

"You're right," Laura agreed. "Evorez most certainly does not know that."

CHAPTER TWENTY-FIVE

V anessa sashayed into the room. She had investigated serial murderers, interviewed bomb makers, taken on terrorist recruiters, and had even sat across the table from a man who had cut off his own penis to use as a wand during a human sacrifice of one of his cult followers. She held her chin up, her shoulders back. "You can do this," she said under her breath.

The smiling face of nearly every parent of the children in Miss Natalia's class turned to her. "*¡Bienvenidos!*" they cried out, while one woman scurried to fill a cup of coffee for her. "Welcome to the parent coffee! It's so nice you decided to join us, finally." Vanessa heard the jab, but decided to let it slip. "It's just you? Where is your husband? He didn't want to participate?" *This is going to be harder than I thought*, she realized.

With those smiling faces turned toward her, she put herself in investigator mode and made her way to her target.

"Claudette, how lovely to see you!"

Claudette's hair was blown out. Her nails were flawless and she had paired a silk top with tight jeans and silk stilettos bedecked with chunky jewels. Evidently, the shortages of products on the street had not interfered with her ability to access J. Crew. "I went to Miami with empty suitcases and came back with them full," she said when Vanessa complimented her shoes. "I didn't have the greatest foresight, though, I'm afraid. I got Cristiana and I decked out for the next three seasons, but I hadn't anticipated some of the more mundane stuff disappearing."

Since Evorez had blocked imports from the United States, shops were emptying out quickly. In the countryside, many people had taken to cultivating their own vegetable gardens, but fresh products in the city were getting harder and harder to come by. Health and beauty products, as well, had become increasingly scarce. Compounding the problem, Evorez had launched a number of sanctions on shopkeepers, to penalize them for forcing people to stand in long lines. "This is a false attempt to run up prices!" he had shouted during a recent television appearance. "They are deliberately withholding products from their shelves and gouging the people of Guayandes!" If he couldn't blame the United States directly, he would blame the middleman. In any case, it wasn't his fault.

"Quite frankly, I should have stocked up on tampons and toilet paper," Claudette said. She said it as if it were a joke, but Vanessa could hear real anxiety in her voice. She leaned in toward Vanessa and spoke quietly. "I'll tell you honestly, it's frustrating." She glanced around the room to see if anyone was listening in on their conversation. "Sometimes I wonder if President Evorez is losing sight of his true aims. I fear he and my husband are too isolated in their bubble. They forget the goals of the revolution, or focus so much on the concept of it that they forget the realities of implementing it. He has a very sound grasp on economics, Segundo. But advising a man like Evorez can be hard."

"Segundo?" Vanessa asked.

"My husband," Claudette responded.

"The president's advisor is your husband? Oh, I hadn't realized." Lying was fun sometimes. "Surely your husband has access to all kinds of products, given his connections."

Claudette rolled her eyes. "He's got access to plenty of things, but nothing that's helping me, and that's all I'll say about that, if you know what I mean."

Ness didn't, but didn't pry. "I have a little secret of my own," Vanessa said. "At the embassy, we have a small shop. I can't get everything, but I did see that they sell," she did a quick, conspiratorial glance around them, "tampons and toilet paper."

They spent the entire parent coffee talking to each other. When it was time to go, they exchanged phone numbers. "Segundo will be traveling next week. Would you like to come for dinner one night? Oliver and Cristiana can play. Will your husband be offended? Would he like to come, as well?"

"He's rather booked up with work engagements, so it works out perfectly." They air kissed each other goodbye, and Ness allowed herself a tiny, internal celebration. *Hook, line, and sinker. I still got it.*

CHAPTER TWENTY-SIX

Victor and Wes stood over a map of Kiltoa. "We're meeting at Anaconda this time. Here." Victor pointed to a small intersection on the far reaches of the town. "Satellite images have shown a lot of activity at the center of town. Add that to the intel El Gordo gave me last time, that the FRPT are streaming in at ever higher numbers, and we got ourselves a counterintelligence clusterfuck." They had been staring at the map discussing possible scenarios for nearly three hours.

"VZSPARKLEPONY knows the day and time?" asked Wes.

"Yes. I just have to signal the location. That means one trip into town to signal the meeting location, and a second for the actual meeting. With FRPT swarming through town."

"Thank you, Lawrence Blackhouse. It may be fitting if he ends up with asylum in Guayandes. I hope they completely run out of toilet paper when he arrives and he can stew in his own shit for eternity."

"I had really hoped we could limit our trips out there. How much time did we spend setting up ECHO so we could avoid this? It's not just the FRPT threat. It's so fucking humid out there."

"Maybe try the Swedish porn vest without a T-shirt underneath this time."

"Is that a map of Guayandes?" Mike stood in the doorway of Victor's office.

"It's a map of Kiltoa," Wes said. "Look. It's a grid."

"I'm putting together a portfolio of maps of the northern region. There's been a lot of activity in the avocado fields there. They're saying bumper crop this year! I'll peruse that map when you're done, if you don't mind." He stood there looking at them for a few seconds. They said nothing. He walked away.

Victor and Wes could hear Patrón coming toward them. "Of course I drank it! He was a murderous drug dealer, I didn't want to offend him." He stopped in front of Victor's door, Adam at his side. Adam looked captivated. "Now get back to thinking about that submarine." He turned to Victor and Wes. "Are you guys feeling prepared yet?"

"I think we've almost got it," Victor said.

"Great. Now I'm going to make it harder."

"Chief?"

"It's almost certain the government will shut down at midnight Washington time. Director has canceled all nonessential travel."

"He already packed his Swedish porn vest, chief," Wes said, pointing to Victor.

"You're still going. There's just one small hiccup. We were supposed to receive a large amount of cash by this morning. But the person in charge of making that transfer left for leadership training before the transfer took place."

"He didn't think to do it beforehand? Or let someone know he'd be away so they could do it for him?"

"In his defense, Victor, only a leader would know to do that, and he hadn't taken leadership training yet."

"Good point, chief."

"With the shutdown looming, everything is on hold. Bottom line, we have very little operational cash. You might have to placate VZSPARKLEPONY."

"I have to tell my source, who is risking his life to meet me in hostile territory and who is already nervous because one of our other operations against the group he is informing on has been exposed by a traitor, that I can't pay him?"

"Try to phrase it differently when you talk to him. That sounds pretty bad," said Patrón.

Victor turned to Wes for reassurance.

"Maybe unzip your Swedish porn vest a little, too."

***

Victor and Wes were loading their gear into the back of Victor's SUV. "Extra ammo?" Victor said.

"Check," Wes responded.

"Batons?"

"Check."

"Double Stuf Oreos for Frank?"

"Check."

"US dollars to pay my source?"

"Maybe he'll take Double Stuf Oreos?"

"Fuck me."

"I don't think he finds you attractive. Although maybe with the vest . . ."

Victor's phone rang.

"Have you left yet?" Andy said urgently. He sounded out of breath.

"We're heading out now. What's up?"

"Meet me at Café Honey. It's on your way."

They pulled into the parking lot. Andy was standing under a tree. His *London Calling* T-shirt looked like it had been pulled out of shape. One sleeve had been partially ripped off and hung down his arm. His hair was pink and stood in messy spikes. His pupils were huge.

"Dude? Are you OK?" Victor asked.

Andy pulled a cigarette out of his pocket and lit it, before reaching into his bag for a Red Bull. He took a gulp without removing the cigarette from his mouth. He handed Victor the can. "That is one fucking crazy city," he said, pointing toward downtown Guayita. He reached into his bag and gave Victor an envelope. "Three thousand in greenbacks."

Victor began to ask how he got it, but Andy cut him off.

"It's better if you don't ask too many questions. The black market works in mysterious ways, my friend. And at mysterious hours. Take it and go."

Victor took the money. "Thanks for this, Andy. Take care of yourself. Try to sleep." He patted Andy's arm. The ripped sleeve fell down a little more, revealing a new tattoo.

Andy took his Red Bull can from Victor's hand and raised it, as though making a toast. "*Buen viaje*, gentlemen. Stay safe."

CHAPTER TWENTY-SEVEN

The tarantula was in its usual corner by the TV. Victor wondered if it had moved in the weeks since he was last there. Three of the four Marias were sprawled on the lobby couch. Frank was still upstairs, which perhaps explained the missing Maria.

Victor and Wes had taken a circuitous route into town so Victor could signal the location for the meeting with VZSPARKLEPONY without drawing attention from any loiterers who might be on the FRPT payroll. It had added several hours to their trip. They were tired, but ready and wired for the evening meeting, which was sure to be a more sensitive operation. They picked at a bowl of peanuts, their watermelon juice untouched in glasses on the bar. The barman turned on the television.

A strong Reggaeton beat blared from the speakers. The two men looked over. Evorez was dancing on an outdoor stage on the edge of the ocean, surrounded by plump women in thong bikinis with the colors of the Guayandan flag. Everyone was singing along as a new campaign song blasted from speakers on the stage. "*¡Viva El Toro! ¡Hijo de Bolívar! ¡El Pueblo unido, jamás sera vencido! ¡Sigan* a El Toro, El Padre de nuestra revolución!" The women gyrated to the music, dancing in a semicircle around the president. Evorez popped the cork of a bottle of champagne and showered the bubbly over the crowd.

"When is the last time those people had access to meat?" asked Victor.

"Let them drink champagne, Victor," said Wes.

"That sentiment has only led to good things, if I remember my history correctly."

After dousing himself in another bottle of champagne, Evorez stepped up to the microphone. "Remember! I am one of you! A vote for El Toro is a vote for sovereignty!" The camera followed him as he waved goodbye to the crowd and made his way to the back of the stage, where an eighty-foot, gunmetal gray, Magnum Marine speedboat was docked. "A vote for El Toro is a vote for you!" Evorez stepped on the boat, fists raised in the air as the two 2,500-horsepower engines revved to life. A giant black bull was painted on the front of the boat.

"It's unbelievable, this show. They're eating it up," Victor said.

"They have nothing else to eat," said Frank. He was in his bathrobe and flip-flops. The fourth Maria was on the couch.

"It looks like a giant floating phallus." The boat sped away. Victor turned to Wes. He shoved his thumb in the direction of the TV. "You see why I don't like Reggaeton?"

"The man in the Swedish porn vest does not get to lecture me on music."

"Are we all set for tonight's meeting?" Victor asked both Wes and Frank. They nodded. "Is that what you're wearing?" he asked Frank, looking at his loose-fitting bathrobe.

"I haven't decided."

"I'll see you at the site. If they try to kidnap me, don't let them take me alive and tell Ness and Oliver I love them. And make it sound cooler than it was. Make me sound like a hero."

"We'll remove the vest before we return your body to her."

"You guys are the greatest. Let's do this."

***

Victor was edgy as he ran his surveillance detection route. As usual, he stopped in a shop to buy cigarettes. He had planned ahead and brought exact change and could see the owner had a few packs stacked behind the counter. The shop was eerily quiet, and Victor could hear whispers coming from the back room. The owner of the shop looked nervous. He took Victor's money without a word before nodding his head in the direction of the door, a gentle suggestion for the gringo to leave. Victor didn't think his presence—the presence of Victor Caro—was an issue. The problem was the presence of any outsider. The FRPT was wrapping its tentacles around the town. The fighters came, found girlfriends and wives, and built relationships with the shop owners. Whereas, even a year ago, plenty of people from Guayita and elsewhere passed through Kiltoa—mostly on their way to eco-lodges in the Amazon—the town now found itself overrun with FRPT militants. Outsiders looked like exactly that: outsiders.

Victor continued his route and approached the meeting site. He saw Wes in the shadow of an electric pole. He could feel Frank hovering in the other corner. He stood in front of a window shop filled with embroidered cloth. He pretended to admire the blouses and aprons. He counted the items in the window ten times. *He's not coming.* He counted them again. *All the time we've put into this case, and Blackhouse scares off my asset.* He glanced up and down the street. *I am standing here asking to be kidnapped, which is a real shame because Vanessa would have really liked that blue tablecloth set.*

VZSPARKLEPONY stepped up next to him.

"You're the last gringo in town, man," El Gordo said.

"We all have Lawrence Blackhouse to thank for that. Has Reis set up a new communications system yet?"

"He's keeping it all low-tech now."

"I guess I better be nice to you. Cigarette?"

"You're looking to get me killed one way or another?" El Gordo took the cigarette. Victor lit it. "It's a problem for Reis, the lack of communication. Many of his fighters have to move much more often than before. They're tired. There's a real paranoia starting to set in. The more fighters are on the move, the more morale drops, the more people abandon the movement. The top FRPT guys are worried about losing people to Tamindo."

"Crossing back over?"

"Turning themselves in as informants. There was a strike last week on a camp a little more north, right after a midlevel lieutenant disappeared. Defections are going up. Morale is going down."

"How's the drug trade?"

"Business is good on this side of the border. It's always good when you have the government on your side. You know Evorez's adviser, Segundo? He likes when business is booming. He's organized a number of Guayandan military officers to help ship cocaine out of the country with the FRPT. They're calling themselves el Cartel Blanco and using official planes and boats to move the product. The planes and boats are integral to the plan. They don't have much of their own. Without official planes, they can't move as much product as quickly or as safely."

"Does Evorez know?"

"Evorez needs the money. The FRPT are happy to share it, especially now that they want to expand their capabilities."

"What does that mean?"

"Reis wants a show of force against Tamindo's military."

"What's he got planned?"

"Missiles. Lots of them. He's getting a Strela missile launcher. Like your American Stinger your mujahedeen used to shoot down Soviet helicopters in Afghanistan."

Victor almost choked. "How do you know this?"

"I'm supposed to deliver the missile launcher and the missiles to Reis."

"How are you planning to get a Soviet-made missile launcher?"

"I'm buying one."

"From whom?"

"The Guayandan military."

CHAPTER TWENTY-EIGHT

The armored car dropped Laura off at the quiet side entrance of the Ministry of Foreign Affairs this time. The media circus had long dispersed, but the bitterness of that day, the last time she had been to the ministry, still ate at her. The minister's assistant escorted her from the car to the elevator and into the minister's office. The secretary was brushing the lint off the red velvet curtains that framed the enormous portrait of Evorez. Laura noted a new statue of a bull on the secretary's desk. On the credenza behind the desk was a framed photo of her with Evorez. The president was looking far away in another direction. She was looking straight at the camera, eyes wide and cheeks blushing, as she leaned in toward Evorez. She had placed rose petals around the frame.

Laura walked through the giant wooden doors and sat across the desk from the minister. He looked tiny behind such a large desk. A small plate of cookies sat near the edge, near two glasses of water. The last time she was here, he had handed her an envelope ordering the dismissal of Laura's boss. Today, Laura had called for the meeting.

"I don't need to explain to you, Minister Flores, the Blackhouse leaks have had a negative impact in many ways," she began.

"I was very sorry to see Ambassador Jones go, but of course, this was beyond my control."

"I am very sympathetic to the difficult position you found yourself in. We've always had a very good working relationship, I believe."

"Indeed, Ambassador Jones was well respected and her positive interest in the local community was well known. I'm afraid the Blackhouse incident complicated things."

Laura took a deep breath. "Yes, the Blackhouse incident *has* complicated things. In particular, President Evorez's decision to offer him asylum in Guayandes places us in a difficult position."

"Ah," said Flores. He reached for the plate of cookies and offered it in her direction. She declined. "This was," Flores paused, "rather unexpected. The Presidential Palace did not inform the Foreign Ministry of its decision before it was announced." He brushed crumbs off his desk.

"We view it as a rather unfortunate development."

"I see," he said.

"You know, Minister Flores, I watched President Evorez's rousing campaign speech yesterday. He is very inspirational. The people of Guayandes are lucky to have a leader who cares so much about them. I was particularly moved by his promise to invest in rural hospitals and schools." Laura paused a moment before continuing. "Minister, the United States agreed to provide President Evorez's government with fifty million dollars in the coming months. This money is slated to help build schools and hospitals in some of your country's more difficult to reach areas."

Flores shifted in his large leather chair.

"It would be a shame if that money could not be released. Projects like that have a positive impact on the people, and I know rural voters are particularly enthusiastic in their support of El Toro, as they should be." Laura leaned over the desk and took a cookie. She smiled at the minister.

Flores took a sip of water. "Will you please excuse me a moment?" He left the office.

Laura put the cookie in her pocket. She knew that money was coming to Guayandes, regardless. She only hoped Flores didn't know that and couldn't read through her charade. She was bluffing. What if he called her on it? She'd look like a fool and likely be kicked out of Guayandes, as well. Not to mention, the United States would look incredibly weak when the money arrived in any case.

Flores came back into the office. He was short and round but held his shoulders up as he waddled back to his chair. "The government of Guayandes is very pleased to hear the government of the United States cares about the health and education of our rural residents, Ms. Pillar." He took another sip of water. "I wonder what will become of this Blackhouse fellow, where he will go." He looked at Laura. "But he is certainly not welcome here."

***

Laura rang the buzzer of the Men's Locker Room and held a bottle of tequila up to the security camera. The door clicked open immediately. Patrón met her in the cubicle maze. "Come in the conference room. It's on TV."

CNN had live coverage of Sheremetyevo airport in Moscow, where Lawrence Blackhouse huddled with several people, as

Russian security officers tried to obscure them from the view of the cameras. Patrón poured out the tequila and handed a glass to Laura. "I guess the meeting went well."

"Mr. Blackhouse had been planning to transit Moscow and continue on to Guayita, the capital of the South American country of Guayandes," a CNN anchor said. "That asylum offer from the government of Guayandes was rescinded while Blackhouse was in the air, traveling from Hong Kong to Moscow. We have now on the phone with us one of our reporters," said the CNN anchor, "who is on the plane that was supposed to carry Lawrence Blackhouse to Guayita, Guayandes. Jeff, can you hear me?"

"I can hear you, Rob. A lot of tension on the plane right now. Several of us from different networks had booked tickets on this and other flights we thought Blackhouse might take. No one knew for sure where his onward destination would be. Apparently, he and his facilitators from CCCP booked several flights to try to confuse US officials. We understand he will not be getting on this flight." A loud bang came over the line. "Ouch! Apologies, Rob. A bag from the overhead compartment fell on my head. A number of us are trying to get off this flight, as well, since Blackhouse will not be leaving Moscow. But the flight crew is refusing to let us leave." There was another bang. "Ack!" Jeff yelled. "Can you put your seat back up, please, you're slamming my knees. Sorry, Rob, everyone is a little tense, as I said. We had all planned on spending the next fifteen hours interviewing Lawrence Blackhouse."

A quiet voice in the background said, "Sir, you need to turn off your phone now. We're taxiing to the runway."

"I guess I'm going to Guayita, Rob. I'll hand it back over to you and the crew on the ground in Moscow."

Rob came on a split screen. Blackhouse was clearly visible. Rob said, "We can see a woman now, standing near Lawrence Blackhouse. We are hearing reports she is his girlfriend." The split screen showed a tall, thin woman with very long hair that was blown out in curls. She was wearing a pink Gucci sweat suit with stilettos. "We are getting information that Blackhouse's girlfriend is a former stripper. She and Mr. Blackhouse met at her place of business."

"Poor bastard," said Patrón. "He actually believed he was so charming that a sex goddess would show interest in him."

The CNN anchor continued, "Lawrence Blackhouse is now meeting with his lawyer, who you can see there in the blue jacket."

The man in the blue jacket had his hand on Blackhouse's shoulder and was talking to him. He turned briefly to the camera.

"That guy used to be a KGB officer," Patrón said. "We had a run-in once in Beirut." He took a sip of his tequila. "I guess he's a lawyer now," he said with a deadpan face.

Laura laughed. "I'm sure he has only good intentions for the former National Security Agency officer." She knocked back the rest of her tequila. Patrón poured her some more. "Maybe we should have let him come to Guayandes. Maybe it would have been easier to control the situation from here."

Patrón took a deep breath and shook his head. "My guess is that Evorez's asylum offer was genuine. Moscow, on the other hand." He gulped his tequila. "Moscow was never going to let Blackhouse go. No intelligence officer ends up in Moscow on accident." He stood up and corked the bottle. "We haven't heard the last of Lawrence Blackhouse."

CHAPTER TWENTY-NINE

Wes pulled into a parking spot near the front of the Blue Wave restaurant. A self-appointed security guard was watching over the cars, part of an unspoken extortion scheme run throughout Guayita. A car guardian would ask for money to guard a person's car. If the person paid, the car stayed safe and the guardian would smile to show what a great job he had done. If the person did not pay, he would return later to find his car scratched from front to back. The guardian would shrug and say, "Perhaps next time you should hire a guardian to keep watch over your car." Wes handed him one hundred chavis.

Inside, he found Alejandro Ramos at a table near the windows, overlooking the valley. Paxico rose in the distance. A small waft of smoke drifted up from the crater. Alejandro was dressed in a sharp, dark gray suit with a purple tie. His black hair was slicked back. He stood and shook Wes's hand. "It's good to see you, my friend."

"How is business?" Wes asked, as they both sat down and adjusted their chairs.

"Despite the ups and downs in our economy, in my industry, we are doing fine."

"Immune from the currency crisis, are you?"

Alejandro smiled and took a sip of water. "There are ways around it. You know that, of course."

Wes did know that, partly because Alejandro had been so willing over the last year to share his knowledge about the business community in the country. He and Wes had met at a conference on Guayandan trade and investment. Alejandro ran a successful construction and logistics company. He wasn't an asset, but he and Wes got along, and Alejandro was happy to share any gossip about the community that he picked up.

"Wes, you and I both know, in the end, every business in this country is living off the drug trade and corruption. It might be indirect, but it's feeding all of us. Every house I build, barrack I repair, product I move, it all springs from the same tainted well. Who are the only people with money to pay me? I recently landed a contract to build a large beach house for a high-level general. Do you think his government salary is paying for that?"

"Are you still building in the jungle?"

"No one legitimate is still building in the jungle. If you see someone building in the jungle, you know who they work for directly. I'm out of that business. But I hear about trucks running through there."

"Who's running them?"

"Usnavy Logistics."

"Usnavy? Is that a family name?"

Alejandro snorted. "He stole the name from the US Navy. As a kid growing up on the coast, back when the US had a big presence here, he saw it printed on boxes and ships. He usurped the name, figured people would think he had a huge supply of ships to do logistics. He's still running trucks up in the border area."

"How do you know that?"

"He poached one of my drivers, good guy who's worked for me for years. They offered him five times what I pay him. The driver told me he's been sent several times to the jungle, just south of Kiltoa, near the Three Caimans lodge up there."

"What's he running?"

"He doesn't know. He told me they had him drive a truck from a warehouse outside of Kiltoa to another warehouse near Three Caimans. All he did was drive. Someone else handled on-loading and off-loading."

"What's up there?"

Alejandro smirked. "I'm not asking those kinds of questions, *amigo*. But like I said, no one legitimate is still operating up there, and in the end, we're all living off the drug trade."

***

Wes stormed into the Men's Locker Room and yelled out Victor's name before charging into his office.

Victor looked up from his computer. "Chill out, dude. Yes, I changed the music, but you weren't here."

Wes looked at him, confused. He listened for a second and heard Edith Piaf droning over the speakers. "We'll discuss that travesty later," Wes said. "I think I found the submarine."

CHAPTER THIRTY

Victor exited the chancery and crossed the compound to the outlying building where the commissary was located. He usually avoided the little grocery store, preferring to shop on the local economy, but he was exhausted from his last trip to the jungle and needed a quick and convenient pick-me-up.

"We don't often see you around these parts, Victor." Ellie was standing behind the cash register, holding a clipboard. "Aren't you usually in the gym at this time of day?" She glanced at the paper on the clipboard then called out toward a back room, "Jorge! You have two orders of Chex Mix on here. I thought you wanted three?"

"How do you know when I go to the gym, Ellie?"

"You usually go around three PM when you're in town. I've seen you."

Victor made a mental note to change his habits.

"Your wife is back there shopping. Looks like she's stocking up."

Victor rounded the aisle and saw Ness pushing a grocery cart filled with tampons, chocolate chips, and brownie mix. "You've given up on the local grocery?"

"The long lines are mostly outside the capital, but I've noticed some shortages here, too, lately. But it's not for us. I told Claudette I'd pick up some things for her, as a favor."

"What a kind friend you are." He gave her a cheeky smile. "Why does Ellie know everything about us and our whereabouts?"

"I think she's kind of the mayor of the embassy. She knows what everyone is doing all the time."

"Jorge! I need a new cash register roll!"

Ness continued, "I'll be delivering these to Claudette tonight, so Oliver and I won't be home for dinner."

"Again?"

"You told me to spend time with her. Every time Segundo leaves town, she's inviting me to do something. We got manicures together last week. Hair blow-outs, too. I can't believe you didn't notice."

"It looks great."

"That was last week."

"I have to eat alone?"

"Suck it up, my love. God and country and all that."

"Before you leave, come by the office. I need to discuss something with you." He grabbed a candy bar, flashed it at Ellie, and said, "Ness will pay."

"I know you're good for it, Victor. Anyway, I know where you live." She paused before shouting after him, "I also know when you work out and other living patterns. My point is, I can find you!"

He waved from down the hall and went outside to cross back over to the chancery. In the Men's Locker Room, he popped his head into Adam's cubicle.

"I'm meeting with VZSURFER again tomorrow. Want to join? It'll be a nice day for a hike and helping someone commit treason."

"Tempting, Victor, but I'm meeting Valentina again. My Spanish is really improving, and I've met some interesting people at the university."

Victor went to his office and sat down. He was proud Adam was setting off on his own and pleased Ness had developed her relationship with Claudette, even if it meant he saw her and Oliver less now. He stared at the FRPT organizational chart and the red Xs. Paulo Reis's photo stared back at him from on top of the chart, his teeth gripping his cigar. Mike walked by.

"We're seeing some huge growth in cacao up north, Victor. There's been real progress converting from coca to cacao. Director's been thrilled with the reports."

Victor turned away from the photo. "Good work, Mike. You are an integral part of this office and we appreciate your work every day. You're a great deputy chief."

A wide smile worked its way across Mike's face and he nodded. "I am, Victor. I appreciate you saying so." He walked off, pleased.

Laura knocked on Victor's open door.

"It's the woman of the hour," Victor said.

"For the low price of fifty million dollars, you too can convince a government whose country is in economic collapse not to offer asylum to a wanted man who spilled our nation's crown jewel secrets."

"If I order now, will you throw in a free flight on the presidential plane for my one hundred kilos of cocaine?"

"You bet! We'll even greet you personally when you arrive in Miami."

Victor realized she wasn't joking anymore.

"Wait, really?"

"I'm meeting with Patrón now to coordinate things on your end. I'll be the main point of contact with the Drug Enforcement Administration guys. I think the boss down there waxes his eyebrows."

"Patrón's got a funny story about an operation he did once with DEA. I won't give it away, but it involves him presiding over the marriage of one of Pablo Escobar's brothers."

"I've heard that one." Laura smirked and walked away.

The front door buzzer rang and Victor heard the door click open. He heard Vanessa say, "Open a fucking window! Do you guys smell yourselves?"

"Always nice to have you visit, Ness," Patrón called from his office. "You smell better than Victor. And all the others out there."

Vanessa sat down in Victor's office. "If we can only discuss it here, it must be about an operation. What's up?"

He grinned. "I have a really great adventure for us."

CHAPTER THIRTY-ONE

Victor sat on a boulder near the peak of Paxico volcano. The sky was a clear peacock blue and he could see all of Volcano Alley, the line of fourteen volcanoes that ran along the mountains, receding in the distance. The air was crisp and cool even as the sun beat down on his face. He had arrived early on purpose, in order to have a few minutes of tranquility and beauty, removed from the cynicism and stress that often accompanies a job in the CYA. He thought about the FRPT. He thought about his upcoming trip with Ness and Oliver. Mostly, he enjoyed a small respite.

He heard VZSURFER, his asset from the Guayandan military, approach from behind a row of bushes. Victor turned to see Fernandez in his usual gray cargo pants and sweatshirt. Victor made to stand up, but Fernandez placed a hand on Victor's shoulder, signaling him to stay seated. Fernandez sat, too. They sipped their water and looked off into the distance. Neither one spoke. On a day like this, the passing of secrets could wait.

Finally, Fernandez said, "When I see this, I can almost forget that my country is in peril. These peaks and valleys will be here long after El Toro is done with us."

"How is his campaign going? Is he pressuring the military to support him more?"

"He's already got the military. Segundo has too many top generals wrapped up in business deals, they can't turn on Evorez now."

"What kind of business deals?"

"FRPT business. The generals are making a lot of money, which is why they are ready to help the FRPT expand even more."

"How?"

"I've been asked to deliver a particular package to a very specialized group of former officers. I believe they will then deliver the package to the FRPT and to Reis himself."

"What kind of package?"

"A missile launcher."

It made sense, Victor thought. El Gordo had said Reis was looking to obtain a Strela missile launcher through the Guayandan military. It seemed Fernandez was part of the plot to deliver it.

"The launcher is going to Reis himself?"

"Yes."

"It will be under your control?"

"I will handle the procurement and will deliver it to the former officers in a town inside the jungle. They will do the onward delivery to Reis."

The two men looked directly at each other for the first time since Fernandez had arrived.

"Are you thinking what I'm thinking?" Victor asked.

Fernandez looked back out at the view and took a sip of water from his canteen. "*Sí*. Let's do it."

***

A few hours later, Victor was back in the Men's Locker Room. He went straight to Patrón's office.

"There's no doubt Reis and Evorez are helping each other. VZSURFER knew about the Strela procurement. In fact, he's in charge of it."

"Sounds like you have a plan for an operation."

Victor nodded, before leaning toward the open office door. "Simon! Get in here."

***

Patrón led Victor and Simon to Laura's office. She was packing up her desk and preparing to head out. "I've got a date," she told them.

"Who's the lucky guy?" asked Patrón.

"The third secretary of the Ethiopian embassy."

"I didn't take you as someone who would date within your industry," Patrón said.

"Ethiopia has an embassy in Guayita?" asked Victor.

Laura looked at Patrón. "Normally I don't." She turned to Victor. "No, they don't. He is the regional Ethiopian diplomat for South America, based in Brazil. The Guayandan Ministry of Foreign Affairs is hosting an official event tonight to discuss foreign investment in their petroleum sector. Evorez pointedly did not send an invitation to the United States. I got myself invited to be the date of someone who did receive an invitation."

"They're inviting Ethiopia to invest here but not us?" Victor said. "That explains so much."

Laura closed up her filing cabinet. "What can I help you gentlemen with? It can't be good. Three of you in my office at the end of the day."

Victor and Simon both looked to Patrón. They had decided he should be the one to broach what was, perhaps, a delicate subject with Laura, considering she was responsible for the embassy.

"We need a place to do a little mechanical work," Patrón said. "No big deal. We've got the tools and everything. We just need a good empty space, kind of away from, well, everybody."

Laura stopped stacking her folders. "Mechanical work on what?" she asked.

"A missile launcher."

Laura pursed her lips and thought for a moment. "It's not going to blow up or shoot something off, is it?"

"No," Victor said emphatically. He turned to Simon. "It's not going to blow up or shoot something off, is it?"

"No?" said Simon.

Patrón looked at Laura with a shrug and a nod. "You see? Nothing to worry about."

"There's a closet behind the garage off the facilities maintenance building. It's not very big, but it's generally away from the prying eyes of local staff."

"Then we're all set here," Patrón said. "Please give our best to your Ethiopian third secretary."

CHAPTER THIRTY-TWO

Victor and Vanessa watched the vegetation change as they traveled from Guayita to the jungle. Over a three-hour drive, they descended more than 10,000 feet, cruising through cloud formations and pine forests into a garden of bright green rubber trees and ferns. Thick vines from kapok trees hung like rope, looking like they would strangle Victor and Vanessa's car as it disappeared under the dense canopy of the Amazon. Oliver snoozed in the back seat.

"I thought going this deep into the jungle was a bad idea," Vanessa said.

"The risk changes from town to town. The eco-lodge we're going to is still pretty popular with tourists. The closest FRPT stronghold is two towns down from there. I needed you to come. A family weekend getaway is a great cover. I couldn't come out here on my own. It would look weird. We won't be the only gringos, and the lodge has an incentive not to allow us to be kidnapped."

"That's comforting."

"It's a family adventure!"

They pulled into a town made up of two dirt roads, a hostel, and small market. Victor parked the car at the hostel. They stepped out of the car and into an oppressive heat. The humidity felt like a heavy wet blanket. A guide greeted them and flashed his lodge credentials, which got stuck in a strap that was holding a machete. Victor introduced himself and his family. The guide gave Oliver a high-five then began leading them down a muddy path through the trees.

They all wore tall rubber boots that sank into the mud as they walked. Oliver's had Batman on them. He wore a rain poncho over his Batman backpack.

"Oliver looks like he's in the FRPT," Victor said to Vanessa.

"Not funny, Victor." She glanced ahead at Oliver, with a giant humpback under his poncho, his boots covered in mud. She smiled. "Kind of funny."

The guide unsheathed his machete and slashed at branches and leaves that had begun blocking the path. He pushed forward and then, with a final slash, the party emerged from the canopy on the edge of the Topo River, a tributary of the mighty Amazon River.

The brown water was calm, but they could hear the rushing of water farther downstream. The river was narrow at this point, and they could see a group of nearly naked children playing in the mud on the other side. The guide transferred their backpacks onto a motor-powered canoe. They headed upriver.

The river cut a brown slash through the Amazon rainforest's green canopy. As they zoomed through the water, Vanessa could see only thick green on either side. It looked impossible to penetrate. She couldn't see any paths or trampled branches.

It looked like a wall of leaves. The humidity settled on them. Everything was wet.

"Those tallest trees you see, they are called kapoks," the guide said. "They can grow up to two hundred feet tall. They help pollinate the rest of the rainforest and are the home of thousands of different species, including bats, which also help spread pollination."

"Bats?" asked Vanessa.

"They sleep in the kapok's many nooks."

"Cool. Bats. Thanks." She looked at Victor. He shrugged. She turned back to the guide. "I'm sorry. I didn't get your name."

"Jorge," the guide said.

Vanessa gave him a big smile. "Thanks, Jorge."

After two hours, the guide pulled the canoe over to the side of the river. Victor, Vanessa, and Oliver clambered out and into the foliage. The guide, a few feet ahead of them, swung his machete back and forth, thwacking branches and limbs as they advanced slowly, squishing through the mud.

Jorge stopped suddenly and approached a giant leaf frond. He whispered, "Come closer."

Victor, Vanessa, and Oliver leaned together and peered over Jorge's shoulder. Perched on the leaf was a tiny bright blue frog, not more than the length of Jorge's thumb.

"It's so cute!" said Oliver, reaching out to touch it.

Jorge grabbed his hand. "Do not touch, young man! This is a poison dart frog. It is toxic. If you touch it, you will die."

Vanessa pulled Oliver closer to her. Victor leaned in toward the frog and said, "That's so cool!"

They continued on the muddy path, which was getting slicker as they went. Vanessa slipped and reached her arm out to grab a nearby tree. Jorge caught her and pulled her arm back in. Once she had recovered her balance, he pointed to the tree she had almost touched. Thousands of red ants were swarming around the trunk.

"Fire ants," Jorge said. "Very painful."

Vanessa pulled her arms tight against her sides as they moved on. She scanned the jungle around her. They were surrounded. She knew it. She could feel it. She could feel the eyes of thousands of creatures on her, creatures she could not see but that were right next to her, hidden under leaves, camouflaged on branches, burrowed in the mud, all within the distance of one toxic frog's jump.

They arrived at the lodge.

The wooden structure was built on stilts to avoid flooding in the heavy rains. It was perched on the edge of a lake so rich in nutrients its water was black. A couple was on the dock fishing. The guide showed Victor, Vanessa, and Oliver to a thatched-roof hut. He suggested kindly that they remove their boots to avoid tracking mud inside.

"Be sure to check them before you put them on again, though. Sometimes things crawl in there," he said. "We also suggest checking your pillows before bed. Sometimes tarantulas enjoy the warmth of the pillows." He left.

"This is going to be exciting, isn't it?" Victor said, turning to his wife and child.

Vanessa and Oliver were both staring at him. Oliver was clinging to his mother's leg. He looked terrified.

Victor was undeterred. "Let's go swimming!"

Vanessa could handle being only a few miles from murderous, kidnapping narco-terrorists, but tarantulas? She had been scared of the eight-legged hairy beasts ever since sixth grade, when her teacher kept one as a pet. It escaped one day, causing a panic throughout the school. One night, shortly after, her brother had placed a giant rubber tarantula on her pillow while she slept. She had opened her eyes to see the giant arachnid in front of her face. Her shriek woke up their parents, who came running in to find Vanessa in tears and her brother doubled over laughing. They grounded her brother for a day, but the incident had left Vanessa with a fear of spiders for life.

Hoping not to pass her paranoia to her child, Vanessa pried Oliver's arms from her leg and put on a bright face. "Let's get our swimsuits!"

The three of them walked out to the dock overlooking the black lake. The couple was still fishing off the edge. Vines hung down into the water. Another guest grabbed a vine, stepped far back, ran, and swung over the lake before dropping into the thick water.

Victor dove in. Oliver did a cannonball. Vanessa dangled her legs in, decided it felt nice in the hot humid weather, and slipped all the way in. They paddled about, floated, and admired the surrounding canopy. They relaxed and enjoyed the sights and sounds of the Amazon. They did not spot any animals, although their presence was evident. They heard birds chirp and monkeys squawk and could see leaves rustling. They were surrounded by life, but it was all hidden.

Up on the dock, Jorge arrived with a bucket for the couple that was fishing. They reached in and pulled out a chunk of something to put on the fishhook. It was too big to be a worm. Vanessa swam closer to look. *What is that?*

The guide saw her inquisitive look and said, "It's raw chicken. It attracts the piranhas."

The woman who was fishing started shouting. "I've got one! I've got one!" She pulled her fishhook out of the water. Hanging off the hook was a small fish with the most enormous teeth Vanessa had ever seen. The teeth looked about half the size of the entire fish.

"Wow! That's incredible," Vanessa said to the woman. "I've never seen a piranha up close." She turned to yell to Victor and Oliver to come see the piranha when a thought occurred to her: that fish had come out of the same water Vanessa was in. *I am swimming in piranha-infested waters,* she thought. *Holy shit! I AM SWIMMING IN PIRANHA-INFESTED WATERS AND SO IS MY SON!*

"Stay calm," said the guide, who was laughing. "They won't eat you. There's enough other food in here that they like better than you."

"And yet, you are standing on the dock and not swimming in the water," Vanessa pointed out.

He laughed and jumped in. Vanessa relaxed and floated in the cool water surrounded by carnivorous fish with razor-sharp teeth, trusting that they preferred the lake's nutrients and raw chicken to her flesh.

Afterward, Victor, Oliver, and Vanessa lay on the dock, soaking up the sun, but never drying off. The humidity stuck to them. As they walked back on the raised platforms over the wet jungle floor toward their hut, the guide called to them from down below. He was standing in a few inches of water holding a large tree branch, which he was thrashing in the water.

"Look, *amigos*!" He pulled the branch out of the water to reveal part of the biggest snake any of them had ever seen; the slithery creature was so large, Jorge could barely lift it. "It's an anaconda!" He stood next to the dark green creature, allowing it to swirl around the tree branch. It had wrapped itself around the thick branch three times, but the bulk of its body still had not emerged from the mud. Jorge seemed unfazed by the fact that the snake could easily kill him. Vanessa followed the water's path and saw it led into the lake where they had been swimming with piranhas a few minutes before. She realized they had been swimming with anacondas, too.

Jorge dropped the snake suddenly and said in a loud whisper, "Listen!"

Vanessa watched the snake melt into the mud and foliage and disappear. It didn't move, it was still there, but she could barely make it out, it was so camouflaged.

They could hear a swishing sound building in the trees around them. The sound came closer, like a wave, growing louder and louder.

"What is that?" asked Oliver.

A group of spider monkeys came swinging through the trees, dozens of them, leaping from branch to vine, from tree to tree, flying through the canopy, swishing past the awed onlookers.

"Flying monkeys!" Oliver was delighted. He gave another high-five to Jorge, who was still standing next to the anaconda, which was slowly curling around a tree.

They continued on to their hut. As they approached, Vanessa saw a dark splotch above the door. She hadn't noticed it before. Perhaps it was a tribal totem to bring luck to whoever stayed there. When they arrived at the door, however, she realized it was nothing as quaint as that. Rather, it was a hairy, brown-and-black tarantula.

Vanessa gulped loudly and stopped in her tracks.

"What's wrong," Victor asked.

Vanessa pointed at the spider. It was the size of a dinner plate.

"That's a tarantula," Victor said, nonchalantly. "Didn't you hear Jorge say they have a lot of them out here?"

"Not giant ones right above our door," Vanessa said.

"The lodge doesn't choose where to put them, Ness." He opened the door and walked into the hut. Oliver followed him in.

Vanessa thought about other challenges she had overcome: blood stains at crime scenes, Lunch Bunch. She took a deep breath, crinkled her face, and ran under the tarantula and into the hut.

That night, as Oliver slept, Victor and Vanessa lay in bed.

"I can check swimming with piranhas and anacondas and surviving nearly being attacked by a giant tarantula off my list," Ness said. "Thank you."

"The tarantula didn't attack you. It was hanging out, minding its own business. It's probably still there."

"Don't remind me."

"You don't want me to remind me to check your boots, which are sitting on the front porch, tomorrow before you put them on?"

"You can remind me about that part."

"If you thought this was fun, wait until tomorrow. Tomorrow is the real risk." He kissed her. "I told you it would be an adventure."

It started to rain. They fell asleep to the sound of the pitter-patter on the roof and the occasional swishing of monkeys flying by.

***

The following morning, Victor and Vanessa checked their equipment. He slipped a necklace with a small device on it around her neck.

"This is an emergency beacon," he told her, as he attached it. "Pressing the red button calls the Marines. I mean that literally. It sends a distress signal and geo-coordinates."

Vanessa patted the necklace, as though it were a gift of pearls. "It's the most romantic thing a man has ever given me." She fluttered her eyes at him.

He put on a waterproof watch with a built-in GPS and hung a waterproof camera over his neck.

They went out on the patio. The giant tarantula was gone. They checked their boots thoroughly before putting them on and headed down to meet Jorge, who was waiting for them at the lake in a small canoe. A caiman leapt from a nearby branch into the water.

Jorge paddled through a maze of narrow waterways before reaching a small path that had been cut through the trees. A truck loaded with inflated inner tubes was parked there. They got in and Jorge drove north, carrying Victor, Vanessa, and Oliver farther into the jungle. A few miles up, he stopped the truck and they trekked to the river, carrying the inner tubes.

"This is where I leave you," Jorge said. "You will see me waiting for you with the canoe."

"What if we float past you?" asked Vanessa.

"I do not advise this," Jorge replied.

The three of them waded into the river. The water was cool, but not cold. Vanessa plunked down on her tube and hauled Oliver onto her lap. Victor was right behind.

The current immediately swept them out and started to carry them away. Jorge waved from the riverbank.

The thick canopy of the jungle again appeared like a green wall on either side of the slice of river. They could hear the coos of parrots and clicks of monkeys communicating. A toucan with a giant yellow beak flew out from a tree, as they floated down the river. Oliver was delighted.

"You don't know exactly where it is?" Vanessa asked.

"It's between the next town and the town where the lodge is. It will be on our left."

"What am I looking for? Will it look like a regular dock? Or a harbor?"

"I don't know. Look for a submarine."

"Submarines are underwater."

"Not if they're docked. Even if it's not there, we should be able to see some kind of infrastructure."

They continued floating. Occasionally they saw a partially built hut or a broken dock, a few pieces of wood barely jutting into the river, but nothing that looked like it could support a submarine. The current picked up.

They rounded a bend and saw it. It was a simple camp: a hut and a sturdy dock, surrounded by a fence. Plastic jerrycans were strewn on the ground. Coils of rope were stacked on the dock.

Victor marked the geo-coordinates on his watch then lifted the camera.

"Smile, Oliver!" *Snap!* He took a picture of his smiling son and the FRPT submarine docking camp behind him. "Smile, Ness!" Victor continued snapping pictures, capturing as much of the layout of the camp as he could. He paddled forward, to get in front of Vanessa and Oliver, so he could take pictures from a different angle, as well. *Snap! Snap! Snap!*

Oliver kicked the water and pointed at another toucan flying by. They continued floating back toward Jorge. Victor and Vanessa smiled at each other. They had gotten what they needed.

***

The following Monday, Victor and Vanessa went into the Men's Locker Room together. They were finally dry, although their clothes from their long weekend in the Amazon were still a stinky, wet mess stuffed in a duffel bag. They'd have to deal with that later. They had a submarine docking base to map out.

A Reggaeton beat was pulsing from the speakers.

"How do you guys work with that all day?" asked Vanessa.

Wes popped out of his cubicle. Victor turned to him, "You see? It's not just me."

Simon stood up. "Did you get it?"

Victor handed him the camera with the pictures of the submarine camp.

"I'll upload them," Simon said.

"Wes, Adam, come into the conference room. We'll walk through them," Victor said.

They sat around the table while Simon fiddled with a computer. Suddenly, up on the wall-mounted screen, there was Oliver's smiling face. Behind him was the FRPT submarine camp.

"I was taking the pictures, so Vanessa paid more attention to the details," Victor said. "Ness, I'll hand it over to you."

"The fence is about ten feet high," Vanessa said. "It's a typical chain link fence. You can see the barbed wire on top." Simon flipped to the next picture. Oliver and Vanessa were flexing their arms. "It's hard to see in the pictures," Vanessa continued, "but the fence continues around the front of the shack, with an opening along the east-southeast line."

Adam was taking notes.

"The shack was wood with a thatched roof. I saw a bench, here." Vanessa pointed to the barely visible corner of the bench in the photo. "I think that might be a foot. Maybe one guy on lookout? Asleep?"

"How about the dock?" asked Adam.

"It juts out about forty feet," said Victor. "It has three cleats, enough to handle, I'd say, a thirty-foot boat. The current is strong. If you're swimming, you have to come from the north. There's no way to swim up that current from the south, even if you're the most special of Special Forces. Same goes for a canoe. A speedboat could go upriver, but it would be loud."

"If they swim, they'll be with piranhas and anacondas," Vanessa said.

"That adds to the challenge," said Adam.

"The piranhas leave you alone," said Victor.

"The piranhas didn't eat you? Are they vegetarian?" Adam asked.

"They are very much carnivorous. An anaconda could be bad if it decided to attack."

"I'll note that down." Adam spoke as he wrote on his notepad, "Everything in the jungle can kill you."

They clicked through the photos, discussing the layout and makeup of the camp, what materials were used, how high barriers were, how it was protected. Simon clicked onto a photo of Victor, Vanessa, and Oliver. Victor had hooked his arm in Vanessa's, pulling their two inner tubes together, and taken a picture of the three of them. The FRPT dock was in the background.

"That's a really nice one," said Simon. "I'll print a copy for you guys. You can frame it and put it up at home."

And they did.

CHAPTER THIRTY-THREE

The following week, Victor turned his attention back to the Strela missile launcher. Adam had taken control of the submarine sabotage portion of the plan. When Victor entered the office, Adam was looking at schematics of a submarine. He had several instant message windows open on his screen. They were all flashing. A banana sat on his desk.

Another instant message window popped open on his monitor. He let out a sound of frustration and rolled his eyes. "Geez, you ask an analyst a simple question like 'How do I sink a submarine?' and next thing you know, you have ten analysts asking for specs on the thing and details about where it's docked. What's it made of? How big is it? Just tell me how to sink the fucker!" He clicked through the different chats, answering each one curtly.

Victor grabbed Simon and Wes. "Let's do this."

As the sun went down, they drove toward the meeting point a few miles south, on the outskirts of Guayita. They had calculated that nighttime would bring more police and military blockades, but also lowered the risk that anyone would give chase when they inevitably ran said blockades. It was quiet in the car and Wes moved to switch on the radio.

"No Reggaeton," Victor said, staring straight ahead.

Wes moved his hand back.

Fernandez, VZSURFER, was waiting for them in a field, leaning against an SUV loaded with the cargo he had smuggled out. Goats picked at the grass nearby. They were not far from one of the Guayandan military's main bases. Victor backed up his SUV next to Fernandez's.

He shook hands with Fernandez and together they walked to the back of the car. Fernandez opened the back door hatch. Victor saw a very large crate.

"That's bigger than I thought."

"It's packed in with a portion of the artillery," Fernandez said.

Victor looked at Simon in the back of his car. "We're going to have to put the seats down."

"Where the fuck am I going to sit?"

"You might have to squeeze."

Simon looked offended. "Sure, make the minority squeeze in with the deadly weapon while this asshole gets to play DJ."

Wes smiled. "I'll buy you empanadas when we get back to town."

"That's helpful," Simon said. "And racist."

"Empanadas are the most common food here. It was a reflection on Guayandes, not you. Besides, you're from Des Moines."

"In that case, you can buy me empanadas."

He got out of the car and put the seats down. They also scooted Wes's seat as far forward as they could. They tried to slide the crate from one car to the other. It wouldn't budge. Wes and Fernandez piled into the front of Fernandez's car to help push from the other side. Wes pulled out a crow bar to give some leverage. Finally, they managed to transfer it to Victor's car.

"We're going to have to do this all again once we're done with the missile launcher," Victor said.

"Why didn't we just go to the military base and let me do my thing there?" asked Simon.

"We determined it was easier to sneak one missile launcher off the base than three people onto the base. You'll have to squeeze in the back, but that's better than getting caught sabotaging a missile launcher on a military base."

Simon agreed.

"Thanks, man," Victor said to Fernandez.

They closed up their cars. Wes folded himself into the front seat, while Simon curled around the Strela's crate in the back. The two cars drove off in separate directions. The goats watched them go.

"Could you watch the potholes, Victor? I'm not in the most comfortable position back here. Not to mention, I am lying on top of missiles."

"Write to the mayor if you have problems with the road quality, man. Does Ellie know the mayor? The mayor of the embassy meets the mayor of the city."

"She probably does," Simon said. "I'm not sure I want to tell her I need smoother roads so I can better enjoy sitting on top of missiles, though."

"Shit," Victor said. "Police blockade."

Simon pulled a blanket over the crate and himself. Wes instinctively put his hand on his gun. Victor looked straight ahead and kept driving. The officer didn't look up from his phone. They drove straight through and exhaled.

They pulled into the embassy parking lot. Wes ran inside to get a cart to help move the crate, while Simon crawled out and stretched, his joints cracking as he stood up. They slid the crate onto the cart and pushed it toward the facilities maintenance area. A Marine was walking the grounds. Victor, Wes, and Simon, hunched over their cargo, smiled and waved.

Victor unlocked the closet door and opened it. A broom fell and hit him in the head. He moved it to the side and cleared some space. Dust was floating around. A single bare light bulb hung from a gangly wire. They got to work cracking open the crate and pulling out nails. The missile launcher and five missiles were packed in straw. Simon sneezed.

"First we disable it, then we put a beacon on it," Victor said, handing Simon his tool kit.

Simon took his phone out of his jacket and fiddled with it. "Sorry, Ellie keeps texting me. Let me turn off the notifications." He punched a bunch of buttons on his phone. It buzzed. Then it pinged. Then it hooted like an owl. "Sorry, I can't figure this thing out." He handed it to Wes. "Can you figure out how to turn it off?"

Wes turned to Victor. "He can't figure out how to turn off his phone, but you are about to let him dismantle a weapon."

"His lack of knowledge about his own cell phone actually gives me great confidence in his technical prowess," Victor responded.

Simon removed a screwdriver and a set of pliers from the toolkit, instructed Wes to turn on the flashlight and hold it just so, and reached down toward the Strela missile launcher.

"Don't fuck it up," Wes said.

Simon looked up at Wes, annoyed. He started unscrewing a panel. He sneezed and the screwdriver skidded onto a missile. He looked back up at Wes. Wes stared at him. Simon went back to work, screwing and unscrewing, tinkering inside, and switching parts. Thirty minutes later, he was done.

"The beacon is attached?" Victor asked.

"We can track it, no problem."

"It won't actually shoot a missile?"

"No. I rigged it so it looks normal. Even if they load it and pull the trigger, it will look like it's going to work fine. But it won't actually shoot the missile."

"Are you sure? Otherwise we all get a free ticket to visit Congress and explain why we delivered a working weapon to a narco-terror group."

"It won't go off." His cell phone chirped.

"For fuck's sake!" said Wes.

They closed up the crate and rolled it back to Victor's car, waving again, this time at the Guayandan security guard who usually manned the chancery's entrance.

"How's Messi?" the man shouted from across the lawn.

"That's my retirement plan!" Victor shouted back.

"Ha! Retirement plan!"

They headed south, Victor in the driver's seat, Wes in the front seat—his nose nearly touching the windshield—and Simon wedged between the missile launcher crate and the back seat door. Victor focused on the road, anxious to get the weapon out of his car and back in Fernandez's possession.

"We're going to Julia's for empanadas," Simon said.

"We're going to Isa's," said Wes. "I once found a hair in my empanada at Julia's. I prefer my empanadas hair-free."

"Isa's empanadas don't have any taste," Simon complained. "Besides, she doesn't have tables outside. And the inside counter is covered in grease."

"You get extra taste by eating your empanada on the greasy counter," said Wes. "That's the whole point. We're going to Isa's."

"I thought the whole empanada thing was for me, since I'm practically fornicating with a Soviet weapon at the moment." The car hit a pothole. "Damn it, Victor! That was my dick! We're going to Julia's. What the fuck is that sound?"

They listened for a moment. The car was making a *whump whump whump* sound.

"Joo fucking kidding me?" Simon said. "I'm cuddling with a Strela in the backseat and you get a flat tire?"

Victor pulled onto the side of the road. He jumped out and looked at the tires. He returned to the driver's seat and stared out straight ahead. The car beams lit up the gravel. Victor rubbed his hand over his face before turning to Wes. "The back right tire is done. *Kaput.* Completely flat." He glanced back at Simon hugging the missile crate. "The spare is under Simon and his mistress."

"We could push the crate out," Wes said.

"How do we get it back in without the cart?" Victor asked. "It's too heavy. Also, I don't want to have to explain what's in the crate if it's sitting on the ground and someone drives by." He looked out at the road. It wasn't a major avenue, and it was late at night. It wasn't likely anyone would drive by. Yet, Victor realized, being stranded in Guayita at night with a sabotaged missile launcher meant for the FRPT—either in the back of the car or on the side of the road—wasn't ideal. He wanted to move quickly. "I'm going to call Andy. He can bring one of the other cars."

Wes helped Simon out of the back while Victor made the call. "He's on his way," Victor said.

The three of them leaned against the car and waited. It was quiet.

"I could really use an empanada right now," said Simon. Victor and Wes glared at him. "I'm sorry! I get hungry when I'm nervous. I'm also postcoital. Look at my Russian lover, hiding under the covers in the back seat. You got a cigarette for me, Victor?"

They saw lights coming down the road. An SUV rolled up, illuminating the three of them. The door opened and the sound of the Ramones blasted into the night. Andy shut the door and the sound stopped. With the headlights facing them, they could only see Andy's silhouette until he was right next to them. He was eating an empanada.

"Where did you get that?" asked Simon.

"Isa's," Andy said, as he popped the last bite into his mouth. Wes smiled at Simon.

"You have to turn the car around. Back up to us, so we can slide the crate," Victor said.

Andy brought the back of his car around. Victor opened the back hatch before Andy reversed the car slowly toward Victor's back bumper. Andy had turned off his music. Victor could see five crushed Red Bull cans on the floor of the back seat.

"It kind of looks like a big coffin," Andy said, as the four of them positioned themselves around the crate.

"Simon didn't mind," said Wes.

"That was uncalled for," Simon said. Wes shrugged.

Andy pulled out a crow bar and they began pushing the crate into the other car. A corner got stuck on an edge of the car trunk. Victor took the crow bar from Andy. They maneuvered again.

They were all sweating. Finally, they got the crate over the lip and it started sliding more smoothly.

"There she goes!" said Victor. "We got it now. Keep pushing. Keep—"

A red-and-blue light flashed and a police siren wailed. Victor, Simon, Wes, and Andy were hunched over the blanketed crate, which bridged the two cars. A policeman flashed a spotlight on them. They froze and said nothing, until Victor finally said, "Shit."

"Keep pushing," Andy said. "Get it in the other car. I've got this."

They gave a final heave, and the crate slid into the other car as Andy jumped out and approached the cop.

"*Amigo,*" he said, leading the cop away from the cars. Victor, Wes, and Simon watched from afar.

"I don't like this," said Wes.

"Give him a minute," said Victor.

They heard Andy laugh and saw him clap the cop on the shoulder, as if they were old buddies. Victor quietly walked around to the driver's side of Andy's car and pushed the car forward a little, so it was no longer bumper-to-bumper with his own car. Andy walked over to them.

"It's all good. You guys should go. He's going to help me change the tire."

"What did you tell him?" asked Victor.

"I told him I'm with the consulate and that's Simon's dead grandmother."

"My *abuelita* is alive and well in Des Moines."

"Get in the car, Simon," Victor said. Victor walked around the car and got in the driver's seat without looking twice at the cop.

Simon climbed in through the back hatch, sprawling on top of the crate. The police officer looked at Andy.

"He was really close with his grandmother," Andy said.

Wes closed the back hatch and wedged himself into the front seat. He looked at Andy in the side view mirror. Andy was chatting with the cop. "Let's get the fuck out of here," Wes said.

Victor had to remind himself to drive slowly. His heart was racing and his adrenaline was pumping. He wanted to be rid of this crate. They all did. There was no more talk of empanadas or Russian lovers. They drove in silence.

Victor turned into the field of goats and saw Fernandez waiting for them. Fernandez looked confused. "That's a different car," he said.

"Don't ask," said Victor.

For the fifth and final time, they transferred the crate. The goats watched them. At last, Fernandez was in control of the sabotaged missile launcher. Victor exhaled.

He shook Fernandez's hand and thanked him.

"Do you think this is going to work," Fernandez asked him.

"I hope it's *not* going to work," Victor said with a wink. Fernandez gave a knowing laugh and walked back to his car. Victor waved and got into the driver's seat. Before Wes could get back in the car, Simon jumped in the front seat. "I'm in mourning," he said, "and you guys owe me empanadas. We're going to Julia's."

CHAPTER THIRTY-FOUR

Segundo and Claudette Espina's house was larger than President Evorez's private residence. It was a bright coral color and was surrounded by a blue wall with an elaborate gate twisted in the shape of a swan. Inside the compound, which was inside another compound, a swimming pool balanced at the edge of a cliff overlooking the valley and the city below and the majestic Paxico volcano in the distance. Oliver and Cristiana splashed in the shallow end of the pool, while a puppy ran up and down the side, trying to get in on the action. Ness and Claudette lay on dark blue lounge chairs. A housekeeper brought them freshly mixed caipirinhas.

"Thank you again for all the goods, Vanessa. My housekeeper told me her husband stood in line for three hours yesterday to get diapers for their baby. By the time he made it into the store, everything was gone. There is so little coming in these days."

"Do they need more diapers? I can try to get some from the embassy."

"You just brought me toilet paper and tampons!"

"I can get diapers for your housekeeper, too. Her husband doesn't have a job?"

"He used to work at Guayandes Petroleum but was asked to leave in the last round of firings."

"If his wife works for you, he must be supportive of Evorez."

"He's not political at all. He's an engineer. His new boss gave him a week to find a new place to drill for oil in order to increase supply. He was unable to do it."

"Segundo couldn't help him?"

"Segundo didn't want to help him. He doesn't want to appear to be giving favors. I try to pay the wife well. The husband gets what he can from the shops, but the lines are impossible. He sometimes pays someone to hold his place in line so he can go to a job interview or get the kids from school. Anything we don't grow here in Guayandes is getting harder and harder to come by."

"I see liquor isn't a problem, though." Ness sipped the lime and cachaça. It was so sour she made a fish face and turned away so Claudette wouldn't see. Apparently, sugar was also in short supply.

"Liquor is never a problem. In any war or economic crisis, people find a way to get liquor. Hair dye and nail polish, too. Have you noticed the women still look made up? I understand silicone breast implants are hard to find, though. One of my girlfriends recently gave in and bought Chinese-made counterfeit boobs. She just had her third baby and decided to treat herself to a tummy tuck and new boobs. Unfortunately, she had to settle for off-brand in this case." She stirred her drink with a pink, plastic flamingo stirrer. "Generally, when you have money or the right connections, you can get whatever you need." Claudette glanced at the house and her property. "You can see we have both. But Segundo was not going to ask around for tampons." She took a big sip of her caipirinha through a bright green straw. "He's away most of the time now, anyway. You know, I fell in love with him for his ideas. When we met, he was in his own kind of exile. Guayandes was under military rule. He wanted to come home and bring prosperity to all the people of Guayandes. He was an idealist. He got a master's degree in economics in the United States. I wouldn't say he despised capitalism. He was concerned about the inequality it could bring, but he very much liked making money. But when it came to his politics, socialism won out. I loved those ideas, too." She sighed. "Now, I can afford a housekeeper, but my housekeeper cannot find diapers for her baby. Segundo tells me it is a necessary step in the revolution and that I should enjoy the benefits we have." She looked at Vanessa. "And we do have benefits! But sometimes I feel a little guilty, you know? He came back from Miami the other day with a string of pearls for me. They're beautiful. But I can't buy toilet paper in my own country."

"He's spending time in Miami? Do you ever go with him?"

"Miami, Curaçao, Panama, and here, too. He goes to Esperanza, up north. That's his main destination these days. I don't know what he gets up to there. I don't think he wants me to know, and I don't think I want to know, to tell you the truth. Cristiana and I have what we need, and that's enough."

"Except toilet paper and tampons."

"He is still my husband, the father of my child, my family." She sipped her drink and looked out at Paxico volcano. "I see the dangers. Don't fool yourself. I see them."

CHAPTER THIRTY-FIVE

Laura stopped at the cliff's edge and looked out over the valley. She took a deep breath of crisp morning air. A long, flat cloud hovered in the middle of the view. She could see the city clearly below it and the snowy peak of Paxico above it in the distance. The cloud floated in between. Her breathing slowed as she recovered from her four-mile run. Her head felt clearer, and she felt prepared. Today was going to be a complicated day.

She arrived in her office, coffee in hand, tossed her suit jacket and purse on a side loveseat, and shut the door. She picked up the secure phone back to Washington.

Thomas Valencia's assistant put Laura through to the man who was her most immediate boss.

"Laura, do you have any idea why the government of Guayandes withdrew its offer of asylum for Lawrence Blackhouse?"

"Perhaps they recognized it was in their interest, considering the damage he's done to US national security."

"I'm not sure what you're talking about. I think it's remarkable, the attention he's brought to the American public about government surveillance."

"Thomas, have you looked through the documents he gave CCCP.org? I appear in those cables three times. Worse, the names of the people I was talking to appear in there. People who had trusted me to keep our conversations confidential. No one will talk to me anymore. They just had a major petroleum event. No one from the US Embassy was invited."

"How do you know you're in those cables?"

"I searched them."

"You searched classified cables on an open network? I should report you to the Office of Security for that. You could lose your clearances."

"How am I supposed to know if the leaked cables will affect my work?"

"You can't look at them on an open network, because they are classified."

"They are available on a public website. The entire world can see them."

"That may be. But as far as you are concerned, they are classified because the US government has not declassified them. So you cannot look at them."

Laura covered the mouthpiece on the phone and banged her head on her desk three times. "Can we move on to the discussion of President Evorez and his participation in trafficking cocaine to the United States?"

"I'd appreciate it if you would include the word 'allegedly' in there. We have no proof."

"It's not alleged if we know it to be true."

"I spoke with Rafa. He loved those flowers I sent, by the way. He's assured me time and again he is tackling the problem of the FRPT. He told me it's central to his campaign and *la revolución*!" He pronounced it as if he were marching in the streets of Havana in 1959.

"Thomas, I sent you intelligence reports explaining the FRPT is using the presidential hangar at the airport in Guayita to fly drugs out and cash in."

"Spying on the host government's president's movements is against diplomatic protocol, Laura. You should be ashamed. Not to mention, it puts me in an awkward position. Evorez only recently asked Ambassador Jones to leave. It would pain me to have to pull you out, as well, were he to discover the United States once again spying on him. He is facing enough battles with his election and the turbulent economy. The people who are hoarding and running up prices ought to be ashamed."

"Evorez cut off imports, Thomas. We didn't cut off exports."

"He had to! After so many years of the United States shoving capitalism down their throats, maybe Guayandans needed a break. I hope you'll rethink your approach to policy there."

"Yes, sir. I'll start composing poetry."

"Wise woman, Laura. I'll look forward to hearing it."

She put the phone down and placed her forehead on her desk, more gently this time. "Gahhhhhhhhh! The money still flows, even though Evorez has coke up his nose. Roses are red, and DC legit, doesn't understand, El Toro's bullshit." There was a knock on the door. "Come in."

Victor opened the door and saw Laura hunched over her desk. "It's better for your back if you sit up. That's also going to leave a red mark on your forehead."

She sat up. There was a red splotch on her forehead. "This other approach you guys are proposing better work, because Valencia is loco for El Toro."

"This approach is going to work. I'd love to tell you it won't involve ego stroking, but I'd be lying."

"You lie for a living, Victor."

"Only to people I don't like. Come on. I'll do most of the stroking."

They went downstairs, through a side hallway, and into the office for the Drug Enforcement Administration. A large plaque with the agency's seal hung on the wall. It portrayed an eagle flying through the sky. Stu Manchin and his buzz cut came out of a side office. He was average height but had burly shoulders and thick arms. They never straightened completely. His eyebrows were perfectly sculpted arches. He was dressed in a tight, black, quick-dry T-shirt, camouflage cargo pants, and combat boots. His DEA badge flashed from one hip, his Glock from the other.

"That's a nice seal you guys got there," Victor said, pointing up at the plaque.

"That's an eagle, not a seal."

Victor eyed Stu's clothes. "Are you just back from the jungle?"

"No."

"Getting ready to head out to the jungle?"

"No."

"OK then. Laura, why don't you take it from here?"

Laura's eyes bore into Victor. She pulled out the intelligence reports she and Victor had prepared for the meeting. "We really appreciate you taking time for us. We know you're very busy and, um, important." She glanced at Victor. He smiled encouragingly.

"This operation is going to be complex and extremely sensitive. But it looks like we've come to the right place."

Stu pulled his pants up a notch and said, "Yes, you did. Come on in and have a seat."

Victor and Laura followed him into the side office. Laura whispered to Victor, "You said you'd be the one doing the ego stroking."

Victor gave her a guilty grin. "I lied."

CHAPTER THIRTY-SIX

Night was falling but Adam could see the outline of the rickety shack, set a few yards back from the river. A large swath of riverside land was fenced off from the road. The shack sat at the entrance to the small dock. Jerrycans, coils of rope, and stackable plastic cartons were strewn across the dock and the yard. It looked exactly as Victor and Vanessa had described it. Behind a row of makeshift barriers, Adam could make out the contours of a small submarine. A short man in drab olive pants and a black tank top with a black handkerchief wrapped around his head came out of the shack. He had a lit cigarette hanging from his lips and a machete strapped to his back. He was pointing an AK-47 at Adam.

Adam put his hands in the air. "*Hola, amigo.* I'm looking for the Three Caimans Eco-Lodge." Adam wore a wig and had grown his beard out. He was sweating profusely because of it. He also wore a baseball cap and glasses, a light disguise. He started walking toward the man. "There's no need for the gun, *amigo*. I left the lodge this afternoon for a walk, but I got turned around. Is this north? Do you know the Three Caimans Eco-Lodge?" Adam's heart was racing, but he kept a cool exterior. Thanks to Valentina, his Spanish was nearly perfect.

The man lowered his gun but remained wary. "You can't come here."

"No, *amigo*. I'm lost. Three Caimans." Adam continued to approach the man. "Wow, is that an AK-47? That's so cool. I've only seen those in movies."

The man was very pleased Adam had noticed his gun and lifted it up to show him. Adam continued to bombard him with questions. The man likely hadn't spoken to anyone in days and was happy to chat. He relaxed until Adam reached into his backpack. He raised his gun again.

"No! No, *amigo*! I've got food." Adam pulled a ripe yellow banana out of his backpack. "Banana? Super fresh."

The man lowered the gun again and took the banana. Adam took out a second one. They peeled them and continued to talk. "Sweet, right?" Adam said, taking a bite. The man smiled and relaxed. He had a small chunk of banana on his chin.

Adam pointed to the stars that were coming out now. "It's so clear out here away from the city. The sky is so much bigger! That sounds weird, I know, but you know what I mean? You can see so much. Is that the Southern Cross? It's beautiful. I guess that means . . ." He followed the lines of the top and bottom stars of the constellation. "That must be south. So Three Caimans . . ."

As Adam distracted the FRPT security guard, four CYA paramilitary officers emerged from the surrounding Amazon foliage. They slid out from under clumps of large heliconia leaves, melted into kapok crevices, and crawled through the riverside grass. One cut a hole through the fence and they squeezed through. They could hear Adam in the distance.

"The sloth is my favorite arboreal mammal. Have you ever seen one? A sloth? Hanging from the jungle canopy? They look like a giant sack of potatoes, hanging out in the trees. They have really long arms, up to fifty percent longer than their legs. Most people don't know that."

The FRPT security guard laughed and took another bite of his banana.

The paramilitary team scrambled across the lawn, hid behind a pyramid of jerrycans, and listened for a moment before scampering across the dock. They huddled against the side of the submarine, their camouflaged clothing and faces blending in with the machine's dark paint. They didn't make a sound. The group's leader bounded onto the top of the submarine in two light, graceful steps and opened the hatch. One, two, three, four, they dropped into the submarine, landing silently and with guns drawn. They fanned out, poking into cubbyholes and hidden spaces to confirm no one was on board. They could hear the river swooshing against the hull.

The team leader signaled his team to hold their ground, and he made his way to the back of the sub, his gun leading the way. He opened the engine room door. Knobs and gauges and tubes and wires were everywhere, but otherwise, the room was empty. He holstered his gun. Then he reached down to his ankle and pulled a knife out of a strap. With two swift movements, he sliced through the hoses of the raw-water cooling system of the submarine's two diesel engines. River water, which normally circulated to keep the engines from overheating, began flooding into the submarine. The team leader returned to the others and signaled for them to go up. He held his knife in his teeth as he climbed out behind them and into the open air.

"I swam with piranhas the other day," Adam said. "Have you ever done that? How come they don't eat you? I had to convince my girlfriend they were vegetarian piranhas to get her to swim."

The team squeezed through the fence and started for the trees.

"Now the poison dart frog, whoo! That's a nasty beast," Adam said. "So cute and small, but those little fuckers can kill you, am I right, *amigo*? That's the amazing thing about the Amazon. You feel these little eyes on you all the time, even if you don't see the creature. Anything could kill you at any time. Kind of makes you feel alive, though, doesn't it, *amigo*?"

The paramilitary team melted back into the foliage and disappeared.

Adam tossed his banana peel to the side. "I think you're right, Pedro. I think Three Caimans is over that way. I appreciate your help." He gave his new friend a pat on the shoulder and walked away.

Fifty-eight minutes later, the FRPT submarine had sunk to the bottom of the river, completely unusable.

CHAPTER THIRTY-SEVEN

Victor threw another log on the fire pit as Vanessa poured them both wine. The sky was clear with the exception of the one spaceship-like cloud, hanging as usual above the city but below the volcano. A full moon shone off Paxico's glacier. Once the fire was going strong, Victor sat down and grabbed his glass.

"How is it going, my little dependent?"

"I'm saving the world, one manicure at a time."

Victor glanced at her hands. "Your nails look lovely."

"There may be an economic crisis for regular people, but the important people still have manicurists come to their homes behind big walls to offer their services to ladies drinking caipirinhas while the children frolic in the swimming pool."

"It's better to be an important person than a regular person. How does someone become an important person?"

"Lots of money, usually acquired through illegal means."

"That sounds fun. We should do that."

"You have to travel all the time, while I consider taking a lover."

"That sounds less fun. Where do I get to travel?"

"Curaçao and Panama. But mostly Esperanza. I hope you like the heat and humidity of Kiltoa, because Esperanza will be worse. You're really in the thick of it. Lots of tiny beasts that could kill you, as well, or that lay eggs under your skin."

"How often does Segundo travel there?"

"Claudette said he is going nearly every week. He goes. She invites me over. It's happened four times now."

Victor smiled at his wife and raised his glass to her. "You do alright," he said, clinking her glass. "For a dependent."

***

"Seriously, can we turn off the Reggaeton shit?" Victor called out over the cubicle farm in the Men's Locker Room. "Is anyone even here?" The Latin beat pulsing from the speakers cut off. Victor waited a second, enjoying the silence. "Thank you." He started walking toward his office. A Britney Spears song started to play. "Oh, for fuck's sake! Who's got the remote?" He went in his office and threw his bag down. Andy appeared at his door. His Sid and Nancy T-shirt was inside out. He had dyed his hair platinum blonde and spiked it up.

"I'm guessing you don't get a lot of pigeons landing on your head," Victor said. "Thanks again for your help with the flat tire. Did everything work out with the cop?"

Andy took three gulps of Red Bull. "We fixed the tire then he insisted on taking me to a club downtown, wouldn't let me leave. I had to dance all night to Jennifer Lopez, Victor. I did that for you."

"Do we give awards for extreme sacrifice? I'll nominate you. That's above and beyond what anyone should have to do. Really, we appreciate it. You got us out of a tight spot."

"Separately," Andy said, "there are some discrepancies in your accounting from your move from Washington to Guayandes."

"That was more than a year ago. Director is going to hound me for money now?"

"The other way around. I was reviewing your paperwork. You moved down here before Vanessa and Oliver. You should have gotten a partial allowance due to the separation. They also should have gotten full per diem and meals for their travel time."

"The support officer at Director never told me about those benefits."

"Because he's not me. I'm a fucking hero of a support officer. I even dance to Jennifer Lopez. You're going to see an extra two grand in your next paycheck."

"Andy, you rock my world."

Andy toasted Victor and chugged his remaining Red Bull.

Victor heard Simon calling his name from the cubicle farm. Victor went out but didn't see anybody. "Where the fuck are you, dude?" Simon's hand popped up from one of the cubicles. He and Wes were hovered over a satellite photo.

"We've tracked the Strela to this area, but it doesn't make sense. There's no overlay with any known FRPT camps or sightings. It looks like cacao fields. Or maybe avocados. There's nothing here, except the missile launcher, apparently."

Victor leaned in and saw mostly green. "What am I looking at? Where are we?"

Simon traced his finger along the photo. "This is the Tamindo border. Here's Tulcano. Kiltoa is down here. This area, where the beacon is, is Esperanza."

Victor looked at Simon. "The Strela is in Esperanza?"

Simon nodded.

Victor stood up and stared into space for a moment. Britney Spears was singing *Oops! I Did It Again*. Victor walked to Mike's office. Mike was singing along and shimmying his shoulders. The remote control for the stereo was on his desk.

"Mike, show me everything you have on the cacao and avocado fields in Esperanza."

Mike's eyes lit up. He rummaged through a pile of folders on his desk. "Esperanza. Esperanza. Aha! Here it is." He opened the folder. "Oh! This is a very interesting field! I've been watching this one." He pulled out a number of satellite images and reports. "The cacao yield must be going up in this area. We've seen quite a bit of activity. Look at this picture."

Victor sat down and looked at the photo as Mike ran his finger along it. "These roads are new. Look at this image of the same place six months ago. This one shows some of the construction equipment. Busy farmers! Like I said, the weather has been good for cacao, so it must be a very productive cacao field."

"The missile launcher with Simon's beacon attached is in that field in Esperanza," Victor said.

Simon and Wes came in and looked over his shoulder at the images.

Victor continued, "According to Claudette and Adam's friend Valentina, Segundo goes to Esperanza regularly. Sergio's intercepts confirm that Segundo is in direct communication with Reis. El Gordo and Fernandez have both confirmed the missile launcher was to be delivered directly to Reis."

Victor looked up at Mike, who looked very excited that Victor was interested in his crop reports. Victor turned to Simon and

Wes. They saw the connection, too. He looked back down at the satellite photo.

"That's not a productive cacao field," Victor said.

He, Simon, and Wes all said in unison, "That's a control center."

CHAPTER THIRTY-EIGHT

Molly Sherman swiped her badge at Director's head-quarters and went down the escalator and across the atrium. Her worn leather bucket bag was strung across her chest and shoulder. A giant plastic bottle of Tylenol inside the bag rattled with every step. Her dirty-blond, curly hair sprung out in all directions. The line at Starbucks wasn't horrendous, so she got herself an enormous iced coffee. She rummaged through her bottomless bag for change, pushing aside the pill bottle, crumpled receipts, an old sticky note with a grocery list on it, and several pens, one of which was leaking and left a black streak on her hand. She paid the barista and used the receipt to wipe her hand. The ink spread across three fingers. She chewed a straw as she walked through the corridor. A man on an electric cart whirred past her. She went up the elevator and trudged down a hallway maze. A traffic mirror was perched in the corner to prevent collisions, as people on foot, or pushing carts, or riding in carts, tended always to be in a hurry in this building full of blind corners. She turned down another hallway and arrived at her office door. She punched in a code, balancing her coffee as her bag kept falling forward, and the door clicked open. She went in.

She walked past the other cubicles, occasionally nodding to a colleague to say hello. She arrived at her work area and stepped over a pile of papers she had left on the floor. Her desk was covered in satellite photos from around the world, stacks of them, piled haphazardly and leaning precariously. A rainbow Slinky was shoved in a corner. An opened can of peanuts was wedged between two stacks of pictures. It all looked like it was about to fall over—the stacks of pictures and the can of peanuts, maybe the desk, too. Her secure phone was ringing.

She placed her coffee cup on the one space she always kept clear for that purpose and continued chewing her straw while she logged on to her computer and answered the phone.

"Is this Molly? My name is Victor. I understand you're the one to talk to if I have questions about imagery for underground construction." After reaching the conclusion the day before that the pictures of Esperanza were likely of a control center of some sort, Victor had spent the rest of the afternoon calling and instant messaging everyone he knew at Director to hunt down the best analyst for reading the imagery. They had all directed him to Molly Sherman.

"She can look at a series of images of blades of grass and tell you which ant just farted," one colleague had told him.

Victor had called her first thing the following day.

"It's jungle pictures? Because anything urban is Mike. Water imagery is Kelly. Don't waste my time if it's urban or water."

"I emailed you the pictures already. I wanted to make sure you got them."

"You wanted to make sure I looked at them before I looked at anything from anyone else," Molly said.

"Yes, in fact, that's true," Victor said.

She put her phone on speaker. She drank her coffee with one hand and typed with the other. She continued chewing her straw the whole time. "I see them here. Victor Caro? Is that you? What am I looking at here, Victor Caro?"

Victor gave her a summary of what was happening with the FRPT at the border between Guayandes and Tamindo. "We think that cacao field might actually be a control center."

Molly clicked through a number of images. "You've got an air strip, about a mile out from the field. And that's definitely tunneling equipment. You see the tire tracks in the mud on photo eleven?"

Victor could hear her clicking away at her computer.

"It rained that day in that location, so if we measure the depth of those tracks . . ." She started to sing the theme song from *Jeopardy* while running calculations on a second monitor. "That means they were carrying a heavy load. The clipped branch on the side, you see that? That's consistent with a Yupi tractor, manufactured in Tamindo. I'm guessing they put it on a flatbed to bring it to the site. The entrance hole is under that second tree from the left. Given the shadow at that time of day and that time of year, and the partial cloud cover on that date, I estimate it is three feet in diameter."

Victor was looking at photo eleven on his desk. He saw a green field.

"Now if we compare that photo with the photo of the area from six months before, photo four, we can see a slight depression."

Victor frantically flipped through the pictures, looking for photo four. He put it next to eleven. They looked exactly the same.

"I'd guess they hollowed out an area about fifty by twenty feet, at a depth of about ten feet. These are estimates, Victor. I can't be specific without proper analysis. Now, what can we fit through that kind of entrance? Major communications equipment is going to need a cooling outlet."

Victor heard more keyboard clicks.

"Yep. That's what I figured. Look at photo eight. You see that palm tree? The third one from the top? Look under it on the right. That looks like a plant stem but it's actually a cooling chimney. See it?"

Victor squinted at photo eight but only saw leaves and trees. "Yes, right there, clear as day," he said.

Molly went on, describing an elaborate underground lair. "There's also been a lot of activity at the site in the last few months, other than the construction. Look at photo sixteen. They're harvesting, so you've got lots of action in the field. That provides good cover for bringing in equipment and people."

"You can hide in the noise," Victor said.

"Exactly. You look at the photo and think people are harvesting cacao. It looks like a banner year for cacao, based on these images."

Victor covered the mouthpiece on his phone and called over to Mike. "Bring me the crop report from November." Mike dropped the report on Victor's desk. "Yes. That field has had increasing yields for the last three seasons."

"If you know you'll have a lot of activity at a spot, you can use the normal activity to cover the illicit activity. I can see here, for example, in photo twenty-one, those are not crops leaving the site. That's equipment coming in, and not agricultural equipment." She shook the ice in her cup, took a sip, and concluded, "If I wanted to build an underground command center for an army, this is how I'd do it."

CHAPTER THIRTY-NINE

The rain poured down but the crowds didn't care. Their rumbling grew louder and louder, like a wave coming over them. "El Toro! El Toro! El Toro!" Evorez stepped out onto the stage and the crowd erupted in deafening cheers. He waved as he walked back and forth before stopping in the center of the stage, listening to the noise, taking it in. A camera panned to a young boy cuddling a stuffed bull.

"How long before they realize his economic policies are going to tank the country?" Victor asked Patrón. They were watching the campaign rally on the television in the conference room in the Men's Locker Room.

Patrón had his feet up on the table. He took a shot of tequila. "I'll hand it to him. He's very charismatic. I'm not sure another leader could pull it off. He can continue to pull it off for a while longer, I'm afraid, using his charm to convince them any problem is someone else's fault. But at one point, empty stomachs don't care who's to blame. They just get angry. That could be in ten years. That could be in ten months."

A television reporter began interviewing the young boy with the stuffed bull. "Tell us how much you love El Toro."

The boy looked to his left for a moment, as though looking for direction from someone off-camera. He turned back to the reporter. "I support our great President Evorez," he said quietly. He glanced left again before turning back to the camera. "President Evorez cares about me and my future," he said. He looked off-camera again for a second before continuing with more confidence, "President Evorez is the leader of the revolution! I love El Toro! He is the greatest and most handsome man ever to live!" The young boy looked off-camera and said, "Was that good?"

The reporter cut him off before he could finish asking his question and declared, "As you can see, President Evorez is loved by the children. He is loved by all!"

Victor and Patrón heard the office front door open and close. "Wes, tell us you have good news," Patrón yelled from his seat.

Wes came into the conference room. He tossed his bag on a chair and said, "VZCUCUMBER confirmed it."

Victor and Patrón each let out a "Woot!" Victor poured more tequila, including a shot for Wes.

"The presidential plane will receive a special cargo Tuesday, bound for Miami. Here are the flight details. Registered flight path, passenger manifest, everything." He threw a pile of papers on the table.

"I'll take it to Laura first thing tomorrow," Victor said, looking through the pile. "We finalized the targeting package and passed it to the station in Tamindo to pass to the Tamindoan military. We're just waiting on the timing." They heard the door again.

"Anyone here?"

"In the conference room, Adam," Patrón yelled, still kicked back in his seat with his feet up. Adam came in and Victor poured him tequila, too.

"Are we celebrating or just drinking?" Adam asked.

"The presidential plane is about to make a cocaine delivery," Patrón said.

"Good thing the FRPT still has a plane," Adam said, "because they don't have a submarine anymore."

The guys all whooped again.

"Did Ness and I get the layout right?" Victor asked as he poured more tequila.

"It was perfect. The team was in and out in the time it took Pedro to eat a banana."

"Who?"

"The guy you saw napping as you floated by. We had a lovely conversation. He thinks sloths are funny. He's probably having a less fun conversation now with FRPT leadership who want to know how their very expensive submarine ended up on the river bottom."

Simon came in. He looked tired.

"Where were you?" Wes asked. "I checked your cubicle when I came in."

"I was helping Ellie print a spreadsheet for the commissary. I couldn't get the damn thing to print properly. These new all-in-one printers are so damned confusing."

"You can't print a spreadsheet but you're sure you disarmed the missile launcher?" Wes asked.

"The missile launcher is disabled. Pour me some tequila."

The front door buzzer rang.

Adam went out and came back with Vanessa.

Patrón grabbed another glass. "You should drink with us more often, Ness."

Vanessa took a shot and slammed her glass on the table. Patrón, Wes, Simon, Adam, and Victor were all looking at her, silent.

"You're the last piece, Ness," Victor said.

Ness looked at them looking at her in anticipation. "Segundo will travel to Esperanza on Tuesday."

"You're sure?" Victor asked.

"I'm sure. Claudette stated it outright. Tuesday. Esperanza."

Everyone smiled.

Patrón poured out more tequila and raised a glass to Vanessa. He pointed toward Victor. "Ness, I told you we like you more than this guy."

CHAPTER FORTY

P resident Evorez sat at his desk eating a plate of empanadas and reading over his victory speech. "We go into the future with an overwhelming mandate. I am touched to have won the support of ninety-eight percent of the Guayandan people." He looked up at Segundo, who was sitting on a leather couch observing a new portrait of a plump Evorez in a sash and surrounded by flowers. "Ninety-eight percent?"

Segundo reassured him, "You won with eighty-nine percent in the last election. It's important to show you have more support this time."

"Can we make it one hundred percent? People love me."

"They do love you, but one hundred percent might look suspicious. We've ensured you will have ninety-eight percent. You need to focus on selling your victory. They love you. Never forget that part."

Evorez smiled. "That's true. I am only sorry you won't be behind me when I give this speech tomorrow night."

"I will be finalizing our agreements up north, which will allow you to implement your brilliant agenda and move the revolution forward. We are all working together. For you and for us."

Evorez brushed empanada crumbs off his tracksuit. *Swish swish!* He looked back down at his victory speech. His fingers had left grease marks on the paper. "Subsidized housing for all rural areas?" He looked at Segundo again. "Can we afford that?"

"After I finalize everything up north, we'll have more than enough."

"For the protection of our sovereignty from the imperialist threats of our swine neighbor to the north," Evorez continued, looking at his speech. "I like that part. Speaking of the American pigs, when my nephews go to Miami with the presidential plane, could you ask them to do a Costco run? It might be a good idea to stock up on a few things while they're there."

"I'll give them your shopping list, Mr. President. Perhaps you should get some sleep. You have a big day tomorrow."

***

The following day, as President Evorez got dressed and prepared to win the election with ninety-eight percent of the vote, his presidential airplane landed at the VIP terminal at Miami International Airport. The plane taxied to its gate.

Dario and Angél Evorez started gathering their bags. Dario put on his white Prada sunglasses and a fedora. Angél rolled up the sleeves on his linen blazer.

"We start at Fontainebleau then hit Nikki tonight," Dario said.

"Nikki is shit, man. No one goes there anymore. There are better clubs to hit." Angél glanced at his Gucci watch. "What's taking so long?"

A flight attendant exited the bathroom. She was pulling down her skirt but the tops of her thigh-high stockings were still visible. She smiled at Dario as she slid by him slowly. He grabbed her ass. She moved along only after he let go.

"Why are you in such a hurry?" Dario asked his brother while watching the flight attendant bend over.

"I want to shower before we hit the clubs, and we have to go to Costco first. Did you see uncle's list? We have to stock up on toothpaste and toilet paper and pens. He also needs a new tracksuit."

The airplane's front door opened. Dario slung a Louis Vuitton backpack over his shoulder.

Angél grabbed his Versace bag. "Finally."

They moved to exit the plane but stopped short. Standing at the door was a large man whose arms were so thick he couldn't straighten them. He was dressed in camouflage, from head to toe. He looked burly, but, Angél remarked, he had perfectly groomed eyebrows.

Stu Manchin stared down the two Evorez boys, as three DEA agents and four customs officers joined him on the plane.

"Put the bags down, gentlemen," Stu said, flashing his badge. "We've gotten some interesting reports about this plane."

"That's a pretty badge," said Dario, "but I'm afraid your pig power does not extend to us." He held up a diplomatic passport, wielding it as though it were a shield. "You have no authority over us."

"That's a pretty passport. I'm very impressed." Stu turned to one of the other agents. "Are you impressed?"

"It's a very impressive passport, sir," the agent said. He stared at Rafa Evorez's nephews. He did not smile.

"The government of the United States is impressed with your passport, too," Stu said. He reached in his back pocket and pulled out a letter. He handed it to Dario. "In fact, the government of the United States does not recognize your diplomatic status. It's a risk you run when you try to smuggle drugs."

"We're on a Costco run," Angél said. "Nothing more."

"We appreciate you wanting to spend your hard-earned cash in our imperialist shops, but that's not going to stop me from turning your plane inside out." He kept his eyes on Dario and Angél and said to his agents, "Search it."

***

Segundo was sweating in the jungle heat, as the jeep bumped over the muddy makeshift roads toward the camp in Esperanza. Vines washed over the vehicle. A large leaf got stuck in one of the wipers. The driver pulled off on a road that had been lightly tunneled in by branches, disguising the path to a tent. Segundo stepped out of the jeep.

Reis, the leader of the FRPT himself, came out to greet him. He was dressed in a drab green military uniform with a matching hat. He was biting the end of a cigar.

"I hope your voyage was not too difficult." He offered a cigar to Segundo. Segundo ran it slowly under his nose and gave a nod of approval.

Reis led him past the green tent in the middle of the cacao field that had been camouflaged with leave fronds and tree limbs. Next to a tree, he revealed an entrance hole, about three-feet wide, with a ladder that led down.

"We only recently finished constructing our command center," he said, as he and Segundo climbed down twelve feet into a large, underground bunker.

Inside, Segundo saw rows of computers and communications equipment, emanating heat, their lights blinking on and off. He noted a pile of small weapons stashed in a corner. He admired the setup, a nerve center hidden underground in the middle of a field. The ceiling and walls were reinforced with wooden planks. A few support columns helped. The floor was covered by a tarp to keep the dust down. He looked at the electrical infrastructure, followed the cables to their energy source, and spotted a small chimney for cooling the system.

"You are rather resourceful, to be able to construct such a bunker out here," Segundo said. He turned to Reis with a smile. "Your work is impressive."

"I am pleased you find it so," Reis said. "We, of course, appreciate the opportunity you are giving us to continue the struggle from Guayandes. We intend to make the most of our stay here."

He led Segundo to one side of the bunker. Lying next to the reinforced wall was a large crate.

Reis stepped up to it and looked at Segundo. "It is a pleasure to share this with you, *Señor* Espina. Your support for our movement has been most welcome."

Reis signaled two of his men to remove the top of the crate. They heaved it up, revealing the Strela missile launcher and artillery nestled in straw inside.

Reis approached the box slowly, as if performing a grand ceremony. Segundo peered over his shoulder, admiring the weapon.

Reis stretched his arms out and kneeled down, placing one hand gently on the launcher's missile tube. He put his other hand on a missile. "It's beautiful, no?" He stared at it for a moment, like a greedy thief eyeing his prized diamond. "This will change the struggle. This will change the revolution. This will change history!" He turned to Segundo, smiling.

Segundo grinned, too, just as the first Tamindoan bombs fell on the camp.

EPILOGUE

Victor and Vanessa stood in the middle of their Florida-themed apartment staring at the boxes that contained their worldly possessions.

"Two years goes by fast when you're having fun," Victor said.

"Let's see. You guys cut off the FRPT's air transport route and their water transport route, and you took out their nerve center, which included taking out their leader," Ness said.

"Technically, that last part was done by the military of Tamindo with your help, but yeah."

Ness watched as the movers carried the boxes out. She closed the door to Oliver's now empty bedroom. She loved arriving in a place, eager for the adventure that was sure to come. She hated leaving. The place that had seemed like home only yesterday now felt empty and strange. The walls were bare. The noise echoed through the empty rooms. A few boxes and tape and the familiarity and life were gone. Yet she knew the transition would be short. The next adventure would begin soon.

"Have you heard from Claudette?" Victor asked.

"I drove by the house yesterday to see if there was any word. Her housekeeper doesn't think she'll come back from Europe. My guess is she's moved back there for good. The housekeeper said she took all her jewelry and most of Cristiana's stuff."

"Segundo was lucky to get out of Esperanza alive. He was next to a support column when the blast went off. It shielded him from the worst of it. I have to admit, I was a little surprised to see him in the background when Evorez filmed himself lying on the grave of Simón Bolívar and doing a séance to try to transfer Bolívar's spirit into his body. Did you see him? He was in the back lighting candles."

"I'm still not sure I understand the séance," Ness said.

"It was actually a stroke of genius when Evorez claimed he had directed the Guayandan military to hit the FRPT camp in Esperanza. It made him look tough on the narco-traffickers and did a good job of countering the accusations against his nephews, even if they are spending the next twenty years in Coleman Federal Correctional Institution for trafficking two hundred kilos of cocaine into Miami. It couldn't erase the damage he's done to the economy, though. We'll see if his charisma and the soul of Bolívar are enough to keep him going."

"Maybe he'll win the next election with one hundred percent," Ness said. "By the way, I heard from Ellie. She and Simon are all settled in Tamindo. Wes, too. He doesn't live too far from them. She's already got a job at the embassy. She told me her boss is named Jorge."

"I saw Sergio as I was packing up my desk. He got a temporary assignment in Dakar, in Senegal," said Victor. "It took him a day to understand it wasn't Dhaka, Bangladesh."

"And Adam?"

"He's staying one more year with Patrón. After sinking a submarine, he no longer feels like a novice. I think he'll carry on our operations just fine."

"Knock knock!" Patrón came through their open front door. He looked at the boxes. "This part always sucks, doesn't it? Here, to lessen the blow and to celebrate." He handed Vanessa a bottle of tequila.

"You know we can't take it on the plane, right?" said Vanessa.

"I guess you'll have to drink it tonight before you leave. You should drink it all anyway. There's reason to celebrate. The FRPT declared a unilateral ceasefire this morning."

"Unilateral?" asked Victor. "Tamindo didn't have to ask for it?"

"The FRPT asked for it all on their own. It seems they've suffered a few setbacks lately that have made them inclined to seek out a peace agreement."

They all smiled at each other.

"It's fun when you see the results," Victor said. "Who's at State in Tamindo to help guide the peace process?"

"It's not in official channels yet, but Laura is slated to be ambassador there. She'll do a fine job keeping things moving in the right direction, if she can keep Valencia focused on writing poetry and not butting in. I've got one other bit of news that is not in official channels but which I already know. You're all getting promotions. Victor, Wes, Simon, Adam, even Mike. In fact, he wrote so many reports, he is considered the top producer of intelligence in Latin America. He's been given a position at Director on the seventh floor. You all deserve promotions, which meant you weren't going to get them. I put Andy on the case. It's done."

"Who knew that food security and cultivated crop rotation in the southwestern hemisphere could be so crucial to US national security?" Victor said.

Patrón turned to Vanessa. "You don't get a promotion, of course."

"You're crushing my dreams, Patrón."

"But Andy didn't forget about you. You've received a special commendation for your contribution. I'd show it to you, but it's classified, which means you'll never see it. Trust me, it's lovely."

"I'm touched," Ness said.

"I'll bid you both farewell. I am on my way to pick up Miss Guayandes. We have quite a weekend planned in the jungle with Frank and Maria."

"The one with the pink—" Victor started.

"Not that one."

"The one who does that—"

"Not that one, either. And not the one with the funny piercing."

"Got it. I see which one you mean."

"It was a pleasure working with both of you, but mostly with you, Vanessa." He hugged them both. "Good luck with the move and your next tour."

"Europe might not be as adventurous as Guayandes," Ness said.

"It'll be Victor's retirement tour. Maybe a little quiet and calm will be good. Keep Victor out of trouble."

Patrón laughed. "God help us all if Victor stays out of trouble."

ACKNOWLEDGMENTS

I have said many times that writing *Victor in the Rubble* was a catharsis. Writing *Victor in the Jungle* was pure fun. Well, it was fun in those moments when I wasn't banging my head on my desk wishing that those words on my computer screen would arrange themselves. I set out to write about the fun and adventure that a career in CIA can provide, despite the absurd dysfunction of the bureaucracy and despite (or because of) the very real risks of the job. I hope this book captures the thrilling chaos and camaraderie that Agency exploits can bring when you've got the right people on your team.

I've been lucky to have the right people on my team.

Thank you to my agents, Judy Coppage and Sam Dorrance, for their feedback on the manuscript and their steady support through my many projects. And a special thanks to Judy, who dropped her very simple words of wisdom—"Just keep going!"—at the exact moments I needed them.

A huge *gracias* to Chris, for his help with the book's Spanish phrases.

To my three chicas, whose lovely faces smile at me daily from a coffee mug on my desk: thank you, for morning walks, afternoons at the playground, nights rocking the crater, and weekends in Miami. Next time, let's go to Des Moines.

I'd like to thank my readers, especially those who let me know how much they enjoyed my first book. When a writer sends her book out into the universe, she has no idea how the universe will respond. The kind notes, the laughter, the acknowledgment that the book spoke to readers' own experiences, and the sharing of anecdotes that would make Victor proud, were oxygen for me. You guys made a second book possible.

I give big thanks to my parents, who instilled a love of adventure in me at a young age and who, time and again, have been game to visit me in strange countries and join me in my escapades, even if it meant swinging high above the canopy or swimming with nonvegetarian piranhas. My brother continues to be a great font of support, ideas, and advice, but I will never forgive him for putting that giant rubber spider on my pillow when we were kids. Thank you to my son for being a great traveler and for joining me on so many adventures. I hope he will continue to make his own adventures. Lastly, I want to thank my husband. He knows why.

ABOUT THE AUTHOR

Alex Finley is a former officer of the CIA's Directorate of Operations, where she served in West Africa and Europe. Before becoming a bureaucrat living large off the system, she chased puffy white men around Washington, DC, as a member of the wild dog pack better known as the Washington media elite. Her writing has appeared in Slate, Reductress, Funny or Die, POLITICO, Vox, the Center for Public Integrity, and other publications. She has spoken to the BBC, C-SPAN's The Washington Journal, CBC's The National, Sirius XM's Yahoo! Politics, France24, the Spy Museum's SpyCast, and other media outlets.

Follow her on Twitter: @alexzfinley

alexzfinley.com

CPSIA information can be obtained
at www.ICGtesting.com
Printed in the USA
FFHW021842150519
52465012-57882FF